HEARTLESS

WITHDRAWN

CACHET

STREET CHRONICLES

Published by:

G Street Chronicles
P.O. Box 1822
Jonesboro, GA 30237-1822

www.gstreetchronicles.com
fans@gstreetchronicles.com

Cover design:
Hot Book Covers, www.hotbookcovers.com

ISBN 13: 978-1-9384424-7-6
ISBN 10: 1938442474
LCCN: 2013931243

Join us on our social networks
Like us on Facebook
G Street Chronicles Fan Page
G Street Chronicles CEO Exclusive Readers Group

Follow us on Twitter
@GStreetChronicl

Acknowledgements

Before I even begin to give thanks to a single person, my first one goes to none other than God, because I am his creation. I'm blessed to be able to wake up each day. I'm also so very thankful for the talent that was given to me, so that I am able to bring the stories in my head to life.

My babies Keiasya, Tre'Maine and Stephen Jr.: you three are the best things that I have ever done in my life! I am so proud to be able to call each one of you my own. You guys give me life, and to see the smiles on your faces give me motivation. I love you!

My Love, Stephen Andres Sr.: I don't think that there are words that can possibly express the way I feel about you. I am so thankful to have you in my corner rooting for me, even when I didn't believe in myself. You are not just my soul mate, but also my best friend. I love you now and forever!

My brother, Alfonzo Johnson: the little brother, who's more like a big brother. You always have my back no matter what and you know I'll raise hell when it comes to you. You can do anything that you put your mind to, don't let anyone tell you different. I love you little bro, tell my nieces and nephew that I love them also.

My baby brother, Dennis Ware: I have watched you grow from a cute little boy, into a handsome, responsible young man. What else can I say, but that I love you more than you'll ever know. I'm looking forward to you walking across that stage, so make it happen. ☺

Antoinette Carter: more of an Aunt then my blood one's are. We may not talk daily, but I know that you're nothing but a phone call away. Thank you for putting me in my place when I allow the naysayers to get me out of my hook up. I love you!

Victoria Kokruda: you are a true friend, if I've ever had one. From the very beginning you've been there for me. I appreciate you and love you girl.

Richard Lampley: my brother from another mother. You've known me the longest, and it's crazy how much you love my little special behind. We go back before pre-school and even though we don't talk a lot, just know that our relationship will never change.

Malacia Johnson-Ware: what can I say, but you're one of the realest chicks I know! You say what you mean and mean what you say, and that aint to common these days. Like I told you, you're not my friend; you are who I consider family.

Chanda M. Carte: it's funny because I've never even met you personally, but I feel like I've known you all my life! Lol Girl, you are what I call a cool person all the way around the board and know everything about everything. I don't know where I would have been without some of your advice.

LaShawne Mincy: one of my closest friends that I've known the least bit of time. You are the most caring and thoughtful person that I know. From the very beginning you've lent a helping hand, whenever it was necessary. I don't say it enough, but I appreciate everything that you've done and will do in the future. Nu Nu has a wonderful God-mommy and he doesn't even know it yet.

Jefferson Branch Library, Lil and Marcy; I love you ladies! Even though I'm no longer there, I still appreciate everything that was done to ensure I had a good read.

My Guardian Angels: Solomon "Butchie" Hill, Darcell Hill, Deborah Hill, Darlene Hill and April Malone. I miss you all dearly, but I know that you guys are looking down on me. I love you!

Kenya Corne' Robinson: thank you for the Ice Cream party idea; my kids really enjoyed it. I told you that I'd shout you out in my next book.

These lists of people have helped me in one way or another. Whether it's been a kind statement, words of encouragement or just to show support while I was busy writing. You guys may not know this, but I'm grateful for those words; they've brought me through rough times. Jessica Harris, Schmeca Ferguson, Destinee Bentley, Dee Dee Bentley, Shawnna Benbow, Sabrina Eubanks, Shawnda Hamilton, Leonice "Boo" Jenkins, Deidre Dailey, Meisha Hill, Jamie Gettemy, Keyanna Bell, Cymone S Lee, Shan Gradney, Marissa Palmer, Nicole Renshaw, Shaleena Brown, Michelle Smith, Lyneeda Dobbins, Qiona Drummond, V. Brown, Tammy Cannady, Pam Phillips, Tracie Pruitt, Hope Taylor, Jessica Johnson, Tameka Galloway, Charlene Gant, Annie Hill, Tessa Torintino, Jennifer Davis, Joseph Bell, Latita Parnell and Tasha Brown.

G Street Chronicles - George Sherman Hudson & Shawna A: Thank you for believing in my talent and giving me a chance to do what I do best; bring that fiyah!

My editor: Thank you for helping me to bring my stories to life. You input helps me so much, and I appreciate all that you do.

To the fans: Thank you for continuing to send those words of encouragement, because even though you don't know, I appreciate you. I hope this book pleases you as much as my last two.

If I've forgotten anyone, please don't take offense. Trust and believe me when I tell you that it's because of my mind and not my heart. I'll try my best to get you in the next one…I love you all!

INTRODUCTION

I done been called heartless, mean, callous, cold, cruel, cutthroat…shit, the list goes on and on, but I, for one, don't give a damn! People can say whatever the fuck they want to about me, but one thing they can't say is that I'm weak. I get what I want, by any and all means necessary, even if I have to step on a few necks in the process. You don't want beef with me, so stay the fuck out my way! If your man is in my sights, trust and believe he's going to be mine when it's all said and done, and ain't shit you can do about it. Either you can fall back willingly or get yo'self fucked up in the process; it's your choice. I ain't gon' keep 'im for long, though, 'cause love is never in my heart. I'm just gonna juice his ass for everything I can get and move on. If you wanna stick around and wait till I'm through running his pockets, you're more than welcome.

Yes, I'm a certified, full-fledged bitch, ho, tramp, slut, or whatever else you wanna call me, but trust and muthafuckin' believe I wear it well. I'm more than likely one of the flyest bitches you'll ever meet, and I ain't just talking shit either. Nothing touches my body that isn't top notch, because a boss bitch like myself can only rock the hottest! This nice, juicy ass and these pretty titties stay covered in La Perla, not Fruit of the Loom, Hanes, or any of that other off-brand Walmart shit you hoes buy. Dolce & Gabbana, Dior, Gucci, Fendi, and Marc Jacobs are shit that I wear on a day-to-day basis. Y'all bitches keep talking shit, but you betta catch up!

Friends? What the hell is that? I don't want 'em and damn sure don't need 'em. I only deal with a bitch if it's beneficial to me, and after I'm done with her ass, she's promptly dismissed. Bitches ain't nothing but back-stabbers anyway. All these hoes have hidden agendas, so why waste time playing games? They just laugh in yo' face and talk behind yo' back to the rest of they fake-ass friends. You dumb bitches have them hoes in yo' houses, all around yo' man and shit, and then get yo' feelings hurt when you catch her with her ass up in the air, with your man giving her the dick! How do I know that? 'Cause I'm *that* bitch, that's how! I'll smile right in yo' face, and no sooner than you turn your back, I'll have my thong down around my ankles with his dick all up in me! I don't give two shits. I'll step on *anybody* to get ahead.

Why should I care about anybody's feelings anyway? Why should I care about tearing so-called happy homes apart? Why should I care that as soon as I come around, yo' man stops doing shit for yo' kids, and they look at you with tears in their eyes when it's Christmas and they don't get shit? It's yo' dumb-ass fault for putting all yo' trust and shit in a nigga. Bitch, get yo' ass up and make shit happen for yourself like I do! My mama never gave a fuck about me, and the only daddy I ever knew fucked me and put me out on the track when I was only thirteen.

I'm twenty one now, and every since I was a young child, I've had to fend for my muthafuckin' self. Nobody ain't ever done shit for me but lie to me and fuck me over. I finally got fed up with that shit, though, and promised myself that it'll never happen again because I'll fuck you over way before you even *think* of doing shit to me. No more crying and feeling sorry for myself. I'll do whatever I gotta do to get what I want, no matter what's at stake! All I got to say is, you fuck with me, you'll get fucked over much worse than you ever intended!

CHAPTER 1

1997...

I jump when I feel something furry brush past my foot. I look up just in time to see a large rat scurry across the room and into a small hole in the cracked wall. The makeshift bed I'm lying on, which consists of two tattered cardboard boxes and a worn-out sleeping bag, does nothing to protect my body from the many rodents that roam about our tiny apartment like they own the place. I hold the paper-thin sleeping bag that covers my body tightly before pulling it up to my neck; it does nothing to stop the draft from chilling me to the bone. I'm freezing, hungry, and scared to leave my room. Why? Because my mama's home and I'm sure she's got company. I know because I hear music in the living room, and I dare not disturb her.

After a while, the growling in my stomach causes me to sigh in frustration. I can't remember the last time I've eaten anything. An empty milk container, which I usually fill with tap water, sits on the floor; my mouth is extremely dry. When I hear scratching inside my wall, my eyes dart over, and fear consumes me. I pray the awful, filthy thing doesn't come back out, but I don't know what I'll do if he does. Hunger pangs shoot through my frail body at rapid speeds, causing me to jerk in convulsions. My aching tummy, screaming for food, causes me to forget about the rat, and I curl up in a fetal position; it's a small attempt to stop the pain, but it's all I can do at the moment. A few seconds pass before I realize it's no use to ignore my starvation. I have to get something to eat, or I'll die in this room and become dinner for that nasty old rat.

I stand up on weak, Jell-O-like legs and stumble, shuffling my bare feet across the filthy floor. When I get to the door, I reach out to grab the handle, but weak and famished as I am, I miss and fall to my knees. I want to cry so bad from the pain, but I can't; if I make a sound, my mama will hear me, and she'll surely beat the skin off my behind. After checking to see if any damage has been done to my knees, I place both my hands flat on the floor and slowly push myself back into a standing position. Back in front of the door, I wrap my small hands around the handle and turn it as slowly as I possible, careful not to make any noise. I stick my head out, and glace from side to side.

To the right, I see my mother on the couch with some man I've never seen before. I'm not completely sure, but I think she may be naked. At the very least, she's missing her shirt. The guy is resting his head on the back of the couch, and his eyes are closed. Mama's head is bouncing up and down in his lap. I'm not sure what she's doing, but the rumbling in my stomach causes me not to care. I hold my breath and pray that whatever she's up to will keep her busy and distracted long enough for me to sneak past her. I tread softly across the floor, but it still creaks under my feet. Thankfully, with the music playing, neither one of them seems to notice me. I keep moving carefully toward the kitchen, hoping to find something to eat when I get there. Anything will do. I'm far too hungry to be picky.

I'm concentrating so hard on sneaking by silently that I don't notice the lamp cord lying across the floor until it's too late. I catch myself, but the tall lamp isn't so lucky and noisily collides with the floor. I watch in horror as the globe on top makes a loud crashing sound as it shatters into small pieces.

"What the hell?" my mother screams. She jumps from the couch in the blink of an eye.

"I'm sorry, Mommy!" I cry, scared to death. But my apology will do no good. I know punishment will come, even if I'm not sure what that will mean this time.

"What the fuck I tell you 'bout comin' out dat room when I got company?" she demands as she walks toward me with her shirt down and around her waist. Her breasts are naked and lie flat against her stomach, and some of her hair is matted and stuck to her face and head, with the rest sticking up all around, looking like a bird's nest.

Tears stream down my dirt-streaked face as I try to explain, "I'm sorry, Mommy, but I'm hungry and—"

Smack!

"Shut the fuck up, all cryin' and shit! Yo' ass ain't hungry. You just wanna be grown, that's all. I ain't no fool. I know what you're up to, out here snoopin' around!"

Smack!

"No, ma'am. I really am just hungry, that's all," I manage to say between sniffles and slaps. My face and back sting and burn from her vicious blows, and when she raises her hand a third time, my eyes close instantly; I know the next smack is coming.

Cachet

"You want me to cook somethin' for you?"

"Yes, Mommy. I would love that," I say, sniffling, unaware of what I'm in for.

"Well, I sho do got something for yo' hardheaded ass! C'mon!" She grabs hold of my wrist and drags me the rest of the way into the kitchen. She pushes me roughly back in the corner and threatens, "You betta not fuckin' move, or I'll break yo' goddamn nosy neck!" Next, she turns the old stove on and grabs a fork that is stuck to a dirty pan. She puts the fork against the red-hot burner.

Meanwhile, I don't move a muscle. I only stand in my spot with a look of confusion on my face, wondering why she's cooking a fork. It isn't until she uses a dingy potholder to pick up the glowing utensil and comes closer to me that I realize what she's going to do. I plead, "I'm sorry, Mommy! I won't do it again! I promise!" I cry out, terrified, backing as far into the corner as I can go, but there is nowhere for me to run.

She grabs my thin arm with her free hand, then places the hot fork up against my forearm and holds it in place, frying my skin like an egg in a skillet. Pain shoots from my limb instantly and goes straight to my brain. I scream out in anguish, so much that my throat feels like its on fire, and I instantly lose my voice. I attempt to shake her off of me, but she has a death grip on my bony arm. The smell of burning flesh is in the air. I open my mouth and try to yell, but nothing will come out. .

"What do we have here, Sophia?" the unknown man asks when he walks into the kitchen, holding his dingy blue work pants up with one hand. He looks back and forth between her to me, trying to figure out what is going on.

It is only then that she jerks the hot fork off my arm, ripping some of my burnt skin along with it. I look down in shock at the charred red blister in the shape of four prongs. The skin surrounding it is starting to peel already, and the pain is unbearable. I give the man a look, pleading with my eyes for him to help me. "Please help me! Save me from my crazy mother!" I want to say, but the words still will not come out.

"Nothing much. Just teaching my nosy-ass li'l whiny bitch of a daughter a lesson," my mother replies nonchalantly, like child abuse isn't against every moral and government law there is. She reaches out and grabs one of my nappy pigtails and begins to shake me like a ragdoll.

My head rocks back and forth roughly, but I say nothing. I'm too busy staring at my arm, trying to figure out how I'm going to stop it from burning.

"Is that right? How old is yer girl?" the man asks, looking me up and down the way a hungry dog looks at raw meat.

"The li'l bitch is eight. Why?" she questions, placing her hand on her bony hip.

"Eight, huh? Hmm. She looks a bit older if ya ask me, only a little thin. I'll pay you triple for a li'l bit of time with her," he said before doing this strange thing with his tongue.

Still clutching my arm, I looked between him and my mother. I was completely confused and had no clue what they are talking about.

"Triple?" she asks, followed by a long pause, as if she has to think about it. "All right, but I want my money first," she finally replies, smacking her lips and holding her hand out.

He digs down in one of his pockets and walks closer to us, then places a few crumpled bills into my mama's hand. She counts the money, smiles at it, then stuffs it in her pocket and pushes me toward him.

The next thing I know, he's got me by the hand, dragging

me over to the couch. I look over my shoulder at my mother, but all she does is pull up her shirt, walk into her bedroom, and close the door behind her.

"We gon' have some fun tonight, little girl," the man says. He smiles a snaggletooth grin at me and begins tugging at my dirty nightshirt so hard I'm afraid he might rip it and get me in more trouble with Mama. And then...

* * *

My eyes shoot open, and I sit up. I lift my arm and shake my head when I see the faint scar, still in the shape of those four cruel prongs. I exhale a sigh of relief, glad to be in the comfort of my own home, all grown and away from that horrible woman. My body is covered in sweat, so much that small beads roll down my torso and onto the covers. *Shit! Now I've gotta change the sheets, and I just put these on! Stupid fuckin' dreams! It's been years, yet I can barely sleep a full night without being attacked by those stupid nightmares. I wish these bitches would just stop already, so I can live my life like a normal person.*

"Damn, 9 o'clock already?" I ask myself, glancing up at the alarm clock on the nightstand.

I climb out of bed and slide my feet into my pink Ugg moccasin slippers and walk my naked ass across the bedroom and into the bathroom. I breathe a sigh of relief as I sit on the toilet and relieve my bladder; my stomach was cramping I'd been holding my piss so long. After brushing my teeth and washing my face, I slide my robe on and tie it loosely around my waist. I grab some fresh bedding from the linen closet in the hall and head back into my bedroom. Still irritated from my dream, I snatch the sweat-soaked covers off the bed, ball them up, and toss them angrily in the corner. Carefully, I sprinkle a nice amount of baby powder onto the king-sized Silhouette mattress before covering it with my burgundy Chinese silk comforter set and matching gold throw pillows. Victoria's Secret Vanilla Lace body spray goes on as a final touch, before I pick up the dirty linens and place them in the laundry room.

My stomach growls, so I hurry to the kitchen for breakfast. I frown as I stare into the open fridge. It's full of food, but there ain't shit in it that I wanna eat, even though I'm hungry as hell! A McDonald's steak bagel comes to mind, so even though I didn't have plans to leave the house till my 1:30 hair appointment, I decide it's time to make a fast food run. *If I only knew how to make them bitches the way they do, I could stop giving them I'm-lovin'-it muthafuckas my damn money.* Inside my bathroom, I glance in the walk-in closet, looking for something I can throw on in a hurry. I decide on a Juicy Couture jogging outfit. In a minute, I've got my robe off and my clothes on. Since I'm only going around the corner and don't have any plans on getting out of the car, underwear isn't even necessary. After tying up my white Pumas, I grab my keys and my Chloé Heloise hobo and head out the door.

Once the elevator makes it to the ground floor, I hit the remote to unlock my doors. I'm happy the parking garage is heated; there's never any need to wait around for my truck to warm up. I toss my bag on the passenger seat and begin backing up to make my way to the Golden Arches. It takes me all of five minutes to get there, but I'm quickly pissed off when I see that the drive-thru line is damn near wrapped around the building. *Shit! Underwear or not, now I have to get out of the damn car. I didn't wear a fuckin' coat, and I know the January weather is gonna rip through this thin-ass fleece.* Impatient as hell that fast food ain't fast enough, I pull into a vacant parking spot near the door, grab my purse, and jump out, slamming my door behind me.

"Damn, baby! You're too damn fine to have that mean mug on yo' face, and that truck is way too pretty for you to be slamming the doors like that," some black-ass, wannabe thug says as he pulls up slowly behind me, smiling and trying to show off his cheap-ass snap-in grill.

"Boy, mind yo' fuckin' business. This is *my* truck, and I can slam this bitch all day if I choose to."

His smile is quickly replaced with a look of shock.

"Maybe you oughtta worry less about me and more about making sure that beat-up ass Cutlass don't cut off on you!" I roll my eyes and walk away. I faintly hear him call me a bitch, but like I said before, I really don't give two shits what he—or anybody, for that matter—thinks about me.

"Welcome to McDonald's. How can I help you?" the elderly white cashier in the stupid brown smock asks when I reach the counter. The skin on her face looks as if it's stretched to the limit, hanging loosely from her face. As I look at her, I realize the saying is true: White folks don't age well at all. Her neck resembles a turkey wattle, that gross red thing that hangs down from their necks. *Shit, if I looked like that, I'd put on a turtleneck or something, because that shit looks triflin' as hell. Furthermore, why is her old ass still on the clock, at McDonald's, of all places? She must be seventy, maybe seventy-five. You'd think she woulda retired long before now, instead of wakin' up at the butt-crack of dawn to feed everybody some damn Egg McMuffins.*

"I'll take a steak bagel combo, no egg, no onion…and gimme a large sweet tea."

"A combo, you say?" she asks, smiling and revealing some dull gray dentures.

"That was what I said, ain't it?" I say smartly, scrunching up my face.

At first she's shocked, but then she peers at me with her wrinkly old eyes, like she's annoyed or something. I stare right back at her with the same expression, because she can't possibly be as annoyed as I am, and even if she is, I just don't give a fuck! *If her senile ass can't hear, maybe she shouldn't be on register—or she should turn up her damn hearing aid! I'm thinking maybe bathroom duty or some shit, but taking orders? No way! The sign says, "One Million Served," and I bet her old ass was here when they handed out their first fucking Big Mac!*

I swipe my debit card and step back to wait on my breakfast. About a minute later, a big, greasy, fat bitch damn near throws my bag at me like she's got some fuckin' problem.

"Well, excuse the fuck outta me!" I say, loud enough for her and everybody else in the lobby to hear (except the old witch at the register, whose ears probably quit on her years ago). I barely catch my bag before it falls off the counter and onto the nasty-ass tile floor.

"My bad," she says, then rolls her eyes and waddles her fat ass away.

I don't understand people these days. How they gonna be so rude to the customers who's payin' their damn measly salaries? What the hell are they all angry at me for? I didn't tell their sorry asses to apply for work at such a shitty-ass place, and that sandwich I just bought is payin' part of her damn grocery bill, which I bet is as huge as her ass! Before I tell the bitch about herself, I walk out the door shaking my head, heading to my truck in a hurry. Honestly, I know that even thinking about that sorry excuse for customer service is a total waste of my time. *That dumb ho is goin' nowhere fast. Besides, ugly as she is, I'd be angry at my pretty ass too.*

I pull into the parking garage and can't get out of my truck quick enough. That damn food smells so good it's got my stomach growling even louder. I take the elevator up to the fifteenth floor, step off, and walk to the door of my four-bedroom penthouse. As soon as I get inside and lay the food down on the counter, I remove my jogging suit and put my robe back on. I grab the sandwich, hash brown, and sweet tea and head to what used to be a guestroom but has been converted into my media room; that's my favorite place to be in the whole glamorous house.

I place my food on one of the four black leather reclining theater seats and put my drink in the cup holder. I walk over to the blu-ray player that's connected to my eighty-four-inch projector screen. I pop in a movie that I picked up from Walmart the other day—Orphan, and from what I hear, it's pretty damn good. I have a seat and recline a bit to enjoy my "dinner-and-a-movie date" with myself. An hour and a half later, I gather my trash and turn off the lights, satisfied that I didn't waste my money; the movie was at least as good as the fast food. *I knew something wasn't right about that little bitch, painting those weird pictures and walking around with that choker on her neck, but I couldn't put my finger on it. Shit like that makes it so I never wanna adopt a kid. You never know what you're gonna get.*

I have a little less than an hour and a half before my hair appointment, and my slow ass needs as much time as I can get. I take a quick shower before oiling my body down all over. I pull my hair into a sleek ponytail that flows down my back and wrap it in a silk scarf. Standing in front of the large picture mirror that hangs in the corner of my walk-in closet, I drop it down low, attempting to fit all this fine, phat ass into my True Religion skinny jeans, putting the stretch denim to a real test. It's one of my favorite brands, but getting those jeans to pull up over my thick thighs and plump ass is always a task. I carefully pull the plain black tank top over my head, then slide into the Kate Spade jacket and tie it off with a belt that perfectly defines my thin waist.

I always make it my business to go to the beauty shop looking my best, because them hoes in there are a bunch of gossiping, ugly, desperate, no-money-having bitches, and I love givin' their sorry asses something to talk about. I remove the scarf from my head just to check myself once more in the mirror before I go. All that's missing is lip gloss, so I reach into my Jimmy Choo hobo and remove a tube of Wonderstruck by MAC. Once my full lips are glossed to a nice, pouty sheen, I blow myself a kiss and close my door, then head out to the hair salon. I was just there two weeks ago, but it was already time for a tune-up. I'm worth it, ain't I? Damn straight I am!

CHAPTER 2

I pull up at Tresses and park my snow-white 2009 Mercedes-Benz 550 right in the front of the window, just to give the hoes inside somethin' else to whisper and roll their eyes about. I hit the locks and get out. I love the *click-clack* of my Jimmy Choo boots as the heels attack the pavement while I strut to the door like my shit don't stink. I enter without saying a word or even acknowledging anyone and head straight to the front desk. Without even turning around, I know a gang of them bitches is staring me down, because it feels as if there's a hole being burned into the back of my pretty little head. I don't even give a flying fuck though; I just add a bit more swing to my hips just to kill them even more.

"Can I help you?" asks a smiling, chubby, fat-faced receptionist, who I assume is new since I haven't seen her before. Her auburn hair is cut in a short bob, and if it wasn't for the acne bumps all over her face, she'd be kinda cute girl. The whitehead right below her chin is threatening to pop at any minute, so I take a step back just in case it decides to; last thing I want is for her nasty pus to end up anywhere on me or my clothes.

"Hi. My name is Brandy, and I've got a 1:30 appointment

with Zema," I say. Zema is the owner and, in my opinion, the best hairdresser in the Buckeye State. As I talk to the new girl, I can't seem to draw my eyes away from that big-ass bump on her face.

"She'll be with you in a minute. Please have a seat." She picks up the phone, dials a number, and says something before returning it back to the cradle.

Zema—and everybody else—knows never to keep me waiting, so I'm sure it really will only be a minute. As I strut across the red and black marble floor, I stare right back at every bitch who shoots me a shady look; I look them right in the eye, letting them know that shit ain't sweet this way. *Don't let the fly gear and the pretty face fool you, hoes. I get down for mines!*

Once I'm seated, I look around and take in how nice the shop is. Clearly, Zema's doing pretty good for herself. The waiting area chairs are red leather and steel, and they blend right in with the black and red décor. A few pictures of models with different hairstyles grace the walls, giving the place a sophisticated look. A fifty-inch plasma TV is mounted in the corner, playing the hottest music videos. *I'm not sure where ol' girl gets her money, but she's damn sure doing the damn thing!* I can't do nothing but give the girl her props; I love to see a bitch handling her business.

I met Zema few years ago while attending LifeSkills, an alternative school for people under the age of twenty-one who still wanna get their high school diploma. We were in the same class, and I remember her telling me that she was gonna own her own salon one day. Back then, I thought she was just talkin' out the side of her neck, but I still listened and let her go on and on. So many chicks at that school claimed they was gonna do this or that, so I just nodded at her and kept the conversation flowing. Now, not many years later, she's doing exactly what she said. I ain't never been a hater, and I gotta give credit where credit is due. Zema's got her shit together.

"Girl, I'm gon' cuss his ass out. I called him when I was almost outta the chair, and his ass was s'posed to be here a half-hour ago. It's cool though, 'cause I'm going out tonight. Hell yeah! I ain't got all fly for nothing," Some butt-ugly girl says loudly while snapping her fingers in the air. The chick she's talking looks to be about sixteen and must be her sister or something, because she's just as ugly—if not more so—than Loud Mouth.

"I know that's right, girl! I'll watch the kids. You know he gon' be all salty 'bout that though," Li'l Ugly says, smiling.

She oughtta be ashamed of her damn self, grinnin' like that, 'cause her mouth is totally jacked up! There're spaces between every tooth, and it don't make it no better that they all yellow as a damn lemonade!

"Shonda did the damn thing with this hairstyle," Loud Mouth says, after removing a compact mirror from a knock-off Gucci purse.

When I look up at ol' girl's head, my mouth drops so far my chin's practically in my chest. *There ain't no way in hell this bitch thinks that shit look good. I don't even know what it is, but I gotta call it a quick weave, 'cause them tracks look like they was done in a damn hurry. Whoever the hell Shonda is, she needs her ass beat, 'cause she didn't even attempt to cover the tracks on that girl's head. That's why I only fuck with Zema, because some of them other so-called stylists be on some bullshit. It's some nice ones in here, but none of them compare to her.*

Cachet

"Come on, Brandy. I'm ready for you."

I look up and see Zema standing there, giving me a warm smile. I get up and follow her to her chair, happy to be away from those loud-mouth-ass bitches.

As we make our way to the back, I notice that nearly all the other stylist are dressed in heels and dress boots, looking like their feet are killing them. Zema is the total opposite wearing a comfortable but cute vintage Mickey Mouse shirt in gray, with black leggings and long gray Uggs. Her shoulder-length hair is pulled back into a tight ponytail with messy bangs, and silver heart-shaped earrings dangle loosely from her ears. For the first time since I met her, I realize that she sort of resembles Vanessa Williams, at least in the face.

As soon as we make it to her area, I remove my jacket and hang it and my purse on the coat hanger not far from her station, close enough that I can keep an eye on my shit.

"What you gettin' today, Brandy?" she asks once I'm seated in the chair.

"I'm thinking of having the crown of my hair dyed blonde, with a short cut on the bangs and straight at the top but kinda spirally toward the ends. Know what I mean?" I ask her after giving her a demonstration of what I want with my hands.

"Yeah. Don't you worry, girl. I got you," she tells me, lifting the chair a bit.

Her smoky gray eyeshadow allows her aqua-blue eyes to pop, and they twinkle under the fluorescent lights as she drapes the cape around me. *I wonder what she's mixed with, because it ain't often you see blacks with natural blue eyes, and I know she ain't wearin' no contacts, 'cause her eyes are always that same color.* Come to think of it, the only other person I've ever seen with eyes like that was my ex, Roger, and he wasn't mixed with a thing—or at least I don't think he was.

Almost three hours later, my hair is done. Just like she promised, Zema got me all the way together! My hair is gorgeous and looks exactly the way I wanted. She even arched my eyebrows and put on more mink eyelashes. I pay her for her services and give her a healthy tip, not only for the hairstyle, but also for the info she gave me. See, she filled me in about her dude's black-and-white party tonight at this place called Onyx in Akron and asked me if I want to come.

I've never really fucked with her outside of her doing my hair, so I was about to brush her off. Then she told me who her dude's best friend is. As soon as I heard "Taz," my ears perked, and she had my undivided attention, because I've been trying to run into his ass for a while now. I went from damn near ignoring the shit outta her to being her best friend, and I told her to meet me there at midnight.

* * *

By the time I get home, after that bad-ass Tresses nail tech got done with my nails, it's already 6 o'clock. *It was worth the wait though, I* figure, looking down at my hands. Shauna's nail art is off the chain, and since hot shit is the only thing I rock, I know I'd be a fool not to fuck with her. The whole time she was doing my nails, my mind was elsewhere. She was irritating the hell outta me, running off at the mouth, talking about her bad-ass kids. I kept giving her one-word answers, hoping she'd get the hint and shut the fuck up, but she didn't. I was too busy thinking about my outfit for the club to pay much attention to her whining.

It's gonna be my night, and I refuse to fuck it up. Hell, I really need this lick. I've only got $137,000 left in my bank account, and I need Taz to help me stack my money back up. My monthly bills are about $3,500, and that don't even include the shopping habit I gotta support. Hell, the mortgage on my condo is $2,900, but I've got $200,000 set aside to make sure it's paid up for the next seven years. No matter what, that money can't be touched, because it puts a roof over my head. I'll be damned if they foreclose on my shit! I ain't like these dumb bitches; my business is always handled first, and anything else can wait its fucking turn.

I pull into the garage, hop out, and head toward the elevator to my apartment. No sooner than I enter the door, my landline begins ringing. I kick off my boots and pick up the cordless, taking notice of the "Private" on the caller ID. I don't usually answer private or unknown calls, but curiosity gets the best of me, and I pick it up anyway. "Hello?"

"Why you do me like that, Brandy?" the caller says.

I roll my eyes as soon as I recognize it. "What do *you* want Roger?"

"I wanna know why you did the shit you did to me? I thought you loved me."

Here we go again with his shit. "Look, Roger, you did that shit to yourself, so don't go around blaming me! You lied to me, remember? So how the hell am I the bad guy?"

"Cut the bullshit, Brandy! I ain't did shit that bad to make you do what you did!"

"Oh my God! What do you want?" I sigh.

"Fine. You wanna play tough? Where the fuck is my money then?" he demands.

I laugh. "Heh. I done spent that shit—every last dime of it! And I'd really appreciate it if you'd stop letting yo' cellies call me on three-way, 'cause we ain't got shit else to talk about.

It'd be a shame if the police was to find out your sorry ass is harassing me, wouldn't it, Roger? I'm sure the judge would love to hear that. You keep fuckin' with me, you're gonna get more jail time. Now, before I hang up, can I help you with anything else?" I ask calmly into the receiver. I ain't about to argue with his ass all night, because I got shit to do.

"Can you help me with anything else? Bitch, I made you, and this is how you repay me? You weren't nothing but a li'l street whore when I met you, sucking dicks for the low, and now you livin' good off *my* money. You wanna try to shit on me? Don't worry about me calling you back, because I won't waste my time or yours. I just want you to know that just because I'm in here, that don't mean you're untouchable. Yo' scandalous, thievin', usin' ass is mine, so you betta take heed. I'm gon' get yo' li'l ass, one way or another! On everything I hold dear, I'ma get you. You hear me, Brandy? You are done!" he says menacingly.

Truth his, his threats give me chills, but I ain't about to let him know he's scaring me. *Naw, fuck that!* "Yeah, I hear you," I reply dryly, "but I want you to do me one favor."

He chuckles. "What's that?"

"Don't drop the soap bitch!" I yell into the phone before disconnecting the call.

I can't believe he just threatened to kill me. I've never heard him talk like that before. I ain't really worried, though, because ain't nobody doing shit to me. He's just running his mouth… right? Grabbing a pillow off my bed, I sit down think about how we came to be. Roger and I had good times. He was my superman back then, and I loved him with all my heart.

Dr. Roger Vines was a fifty-four-year-old cosmetic surgeon who was paid the big bucks to work on some of the most famous people in the world. He'd been practicing for fifteen years and had huge offices in California and Florida, as well as a small one in Ohio. Of course, his offices in the sunnier states where the celebrities live did the most business, but he did plenty of liposuctions and breast lifts on Midwestern clients too. A few times, he even took business trips to places like Spain, Brazil, and Greece; it was worth the trip to do a few $100,000 jobs. To say he was on his shit would be an understatement.

I thought he was the one, the man I'd marry, but I came to find out he was deceiving me. Even now, I can't believe he lied to me the way he did, but it goes back to what I always say: You can't trust anybody. I believe Roger was the straw who broke this camel's back, as they say, because after he did me wrong, I've been malicious every since. Nobody would've been able to tell me back then that we'd be where we are today. I had to learn the hard way that the man's words and promises were about as fake as the faces of his Botox patients.

* * *

2004…

A car speeding a little too close to the curb hits a puddle, and I jump back in an attempt to stop the cold, dirty water from drenching me. It just barely misses my body but comes in contact with my black legwarmers that cover a pair of well-worn heels, instantly freezing my feet. "Stupid bitch!" I yell as the back lights disappear down the street. I hate drivers like that, and I'm sure she saw all that damn water on the ground.

It's a cold March day, and if I were any other fifteen-year-old female, I wouldn't have any business standing downtown in front of the North Point Inn, waiting on my next trick, but this is my life. My father/pimp, Pitch, don't play when it comes to money, so I'm forced to stand outside in the arctic-like cold with barely a stitch of clothing on my young body, lookin' like the whore he's made me out to be. My hands are stuffed inside the pockets of a small bubble coat that hardly manages to keep the wind out, and my nipples feel like ice cubes under the only other layer of fabric, a thin tank. In an attempt to keep myself from dying of hypothermia, I bounce from my left leg to my right; it's pointless, because the sheer black leggings are so tight and thin that they're damn near transparent, and the wind rips right through them.

I bat my eyes in surprise when a pretty-ass black and chrome Mercedes-Benz pulls up and stops directly in front of me. All the girls scramble and shit, hoping it's there for one of them. The window rolls down slowly, and before he says a word, I've already got my mind made up that he's a cop, because there's no way a man like that would be in the 'hood looking for a trick. With his ring-clad and perfectly manicured finger, he motions me over, but I don't budge; if he is the police, I know Pitch would have my ass in a sling for dumbly getting arrested.

"You there, in the black pants, come here," he finally says.

I slowly walk over to his truck, straining my eyes to see inside. I notice that he resembles an older version of Idris Elba, he's the guy who played Russell on The Wire, *an HBO show. "You the police?" I asked, peering at him suspiciously, wondering how such a chocolate man had such blue eyes.*

"No, but I want you to take a ride with me. Hop in." As soon as the words leave his lips, the black-tinted window rolls up, and I hear the faint click *of the automatic locks opening to let me in.*

Cachet

"So, what can I do for you today? The full package'll be $125, and I'll need that up front," I tell him as soon as I climb into his truck.

"I don't want to have sex with you," he tells me with a hard look on his face.

The words hit me like a ton of brinks, and I wonder what I'm doing in his truck if he doesn't want me for sex. I worry for a moment about what he plans to do to me. The thought of being tortured and killed pops into my mind, and I reach out and grab the door handle just in case I have to dip on his ass.

I figure he must have noticed the look on my face, because his eyes soften and he continues, "I just want to talk to you. Will this cover that?" he asks, tossing a roll of money in my lap.

I quickly count it with my eyes and realize he just handed me over $5,000. A few seconds later, I exhale, not even aware that I've been holding my breath the whole time. "Mister, I don't know who you are, but I do know damn well that nobody's gonna give me five stacks just to sit here and talk. Don't play fucking games with me, man. What do you really want?" I ask, irritated. I'm sure he wants to do some hella freaky shit for five Gs, and I don't know if I'm up for that.

"Like I said, I only want to talk," he tells me sincerely.

I shrug. "All right, mister. Whatever you say. It's your money."

We sit in his fancy-ass truck for hours, talking about everything under the sun. I soon discover that he's cool as hell and down to Earth. By the looks of his suit, I at first thought he'd be the uptight type, but when we started talking, he made me feel right at home.

It comes time for him to drop me off, and I can't lie: I don't want to go back. That little bit of time while I sat with him made me feel like a human being again, not just some trick who fucks and sucks for a living. When we pull up in front of the hotel where he picked me up in the first place, he thanks me for my time. I get out slowly and stomp back toward my post.

For the next six months, he starts coming around weekly, and all he wants to do is talk. We go to restaurants just to grab a bite to eat or just sit at the park and chop it up. He's a great listener when I need it, and as time goes on, I open up more and more, letting him know my deepest, darkest secrets. No matter what I tell him, he never flinches or looks at me any different. He just tells me over and over how much he enjoys talking to me, and he often asks about my plans for the future. At first, I told him I couldn't see past tricking, but at fifteen, my body's getting tired of it. My poor little pussy has more miles on it than a drug mule's car. Even when I tell him that, it doesn't seem to bother him. He just says my past doesn't count and that my future is still bright, even after all the shit I've been though.

I can't do nothing but laugh and tell him he's crazy to think a girl who started selling her pussy since the tender age of eight has any kind of future. There damn sure ain't no Social Security checks for a retired ho! He just says he knows for a fact that there's more for me out there and that if I put my trust in him, he'll make sure I have everything and more. That's all peaches and cream, but I don't trust a muthafuckin' soul. Why would I? I used to trust Mama, and she damn near starved me to death, burned me with a fucking fork, and sold me to the dope man when I was eight. I'm almost glad she died when I was twelve so I ain't have to put up with her sorry ass no more. Since then, I've had to live with my daddy, Pitch. He claimed

Cachet

he loved me and promised to treat me like his li'l princess, but it sho didn't take him long to put me out on the ho stroll when I was thirteen. Since then, I've made it my business not to put my faith in anyone, no matter who they are. If you ask me, everybody's after something.

After six months, even he stops coming around. Just like I suspected, I couldn't trust him either.

* * *

My sixteenth birthday just passed, and I'm one year closer to being grown. It's nippy outside, and the heels I'm wearing are killing my feet. I can't believe my eyes when I see his truck pull up, 'cause it's been six months since I seen him last. I'm so happy to see him that I can't hardly contain myself. I figured he'd gotten tired of talking to my miserable ass and kept it moving. Truthfully, I wouldn't have blamed him.

"Hey there, beautiful. Get in," he says to me.

His smile causes me to melt. His chocolate skin looks so good against the white, button-up shirt he's wearing, and he has this look about him that just screams, "Money!" Truly, the man is fine as hell, and I'm beginning to think I'd like to do more with him than talk.

I climb in his truck without a second thought. Instantly, my shivering thighs melt against the heated leather seats. I smile when I realize he already had them on for me. He's always been caring like that. He gives me that look, and I know I have to clasp my seatbelt before he'll pull off. He's always looking after me whenever he's around.

"Where the hell you been?" I ask once we're in motion.

"Hush. I've got a surprise for you," he answers. He then maneuvers us through the city of Cleveland.

Not another word escapes my lips, and I sit back and enjoy the ride, wondering what he has in store for me.

I must've dozed off, because the next thing I feel is him shaking me awake. When my eyes finally come into focus, I notice that we're parked in front of an apartment complex, Dover Farms Luxury Apartments. The buildings appear to be three stories, and I figure this is where he lives and that today's the day I'll have to give up some pussy for all the money he's invested in me. Honestly, I'm not even mad about it. Like I said before, I've been wanting to fuck him for a while.

"C'mon," he says, opening the door for me like I'm some kind of good and proper lady who deserves a gentleman.

I hop out of the truck and follow him to one of the cream and brick buildings, up the staircase, and straight to an apartment door on the second floor; he sticks in a key and opens it.

When we step inside, I'm immediately impressed with the décor. The first thing I notice is the huge picture of an African-American angel above the fireplace in the living room. She has a glowing halo above her head, and she's embracing herself. I'm not exactly sure what the artist thinks it should represent, but in my opinion, it's a symbol of strength. Glancing over the rest of the area, I notice that two of the four walls in the living room are white, while the other two are painted a bright orange color. There is a white, three-piece furniture set, decorated with throw pillows the exact same color orange as the walls. Those two colors spill over into the small dining room to the left, furnished with a white table and orange chairs. It's perfectly color coordinated and beautiful.

"Well? What do you think?"

"Very nice. Do you live here alone?"

"Huh?" He chuckles. "Brandy, this isn't my house."

Cachet

"It's not?" I question, confused. "Then whose is it, and what are we doing here?"

"Well, we've known each other for so long I didn't think you'd mind us coming back to your place for a while?"

"What?" I ask, unable to believe what he was getting at. "My place?"

"Yes, Brandy. It's about time you have your own place, and you need to get away from that awful Pitch. I had to wait till you were a little older so it won't be a problem for you to live here alone, but now it's all yours."

Still skeptical of anybody ever being so kind, I ask, "What do I gotta do for it?" I ain't no damn fool, and I know men—especially the wealthy ones—don't just give a girl shit without expecting something in return.

"All you have to do is promise me that you'll go to school to learn some kind of trade so you can better yourself." His blue eyes seem as if they're staring into my very soul when he says it; nobody's ever looked at me like that before. When I don't answer right away, 'cause I'm too stunned to speak, he runs his hand across his salt-and-pepper beard, as if he's in deep thought. "Brandy, the truth is, I don't want anything from you that you don't want to give me. I will make sure your bills are paid and that you have money in your pocket, and all I want in return is for you to let me be the one who makes you happy."

Still not sure what he's up to, I ask, "What are you saying, Roger?"

"I'm saying I want to be with you. I want to be the man who provides everything you need. I want to be the one to spoil you, to love you."

Utterly confused, I shake my head from left to right. "I-I

don't know, Roger. I'm only sixteen, and I can't really repay you." I stutter, barely able to digest everything that's happening.

"I don't want anything from you but your heart. Just tell me you'll think about it. If you decide to stay, we can go out and get you a car right away."

I'm at a loss for words and can't think of anything to say to this man who's attempting to give me everything I've ever wanted. I'm happy knowing I can finally get away from Pitch and his bullshit, but I'm also scared. Every time I trust someone, I end up getting hurt. "But...how do I know this is real?" I ask with tears in my eyes.

"Because I give you my word," is all he says.

* * *

My phone rings, and I'm awakened from my accidental nap by Jamie Foxx's "Blame It." I look at the caller ID and realize it's Zema. "What's up?" I ask after I slide the green phone button over on my T-Mobile G1.

"Hey, Brandy, you wanna ride with me to the party?"

I roll my eyes. *This bitch is really tripping. What the fuck I look like riding with a bitch to a bar when I'm trying to snag a nigga? Plus, me and this bitch ain't even friends for real. I'm only using her to get to Taz.* "Naw, I'm good. I'll drive myself, 'cause I ain't even ready yet," I tell her, and it's the truth; I haven't even washed my ass yet.

"I ain't either. Maybe I can come over to your house, and we can get dressed and leave together," she rambles in a pathetic attempt to be my friend.

Get dressed at my place and leave together? What the fuck? How old does she think I am, sixteen? Next thing I know, she'll be wanting to have a damn slumber party. "Uh, we could do that, but my dude is here, and you know what that means. I'll just meet you there okay?"

"Oh…okay, girl. Do yo' thang. I'll see you at the party."

"All right." It's a shame I had to lie to the ho, but I had to get her to let up with that best buddies shit, 'cause that ain't what I'm in the market for.

I jump off the bed and hurry to the bathroom to shower. I want to make an appearance, but I don't want to be so late that Taz is already busy, gettin' up in another bitch's face. *Yeah, I've got first dibs on that shit, whether he knows it yet or not.*

CHAPTER 3

When I pull up at Onyx, I'm relieved to find a parking spot directly across the street from the door. I woulda been mad as fuck if I'da had to walk from clear down that long-ass street! It's packed as hell, and for the life of me, I can't figure out why they don't have a valet. As I scan the front of the building, I see that the line is practically going around the corner, and I know there ain't no way in hell I'm standing out in the freezing cold like those fools. I lock my doors and walk straight up to the front of the line. Like I told you, I'm that bitch!

"Excuse me!" some busted bitch with a part that looks to be about a mile long in her invisible quick weave yells.

I almost go in on her, but by the looks of things, life has been cruel enough to her already. She's wearing a pair of fake-ass leather pants that look like they're about to bust at the seams any minute because of her big-ass thighs; they're so tight I can see her cottage cheese-looking cellulite through the fabric. The three-quarter-inch matching jacket doesn't look any better, because her broad, linebacker shoulders are stretching that poor fabric to its ultimate limit. A too-small baby tee shows doesn't showcase anything but her protruding, stretch-marked stomach every time she breathes. On top of that, she looks like she's bow-legged, but then I realize it's her thrift-store-looking boots; one of the heels is so worn down that it makes her lean to one side, and I wonder how the hell she can even walk in those things. I ignore her remark, and so does the bouncer as he grants me access to the club without a second thought. She's still talking shit as I strut in, but I don't even bother to acknowledge her dumb ass.

As I head toward the bar, I notice that damn near every nigga in the place is breaking his neck to get a look at the pretty bitch with the nice body—meaning me. The white St. John sequined tank I'm wearing under my black Valentino seamed leather jacket does little to hide my plump-ass booty that I've squeezed into my 7 for All Mankind Second Skin skinny jeans. With every step I take, my ass bounces from left to right, and even though I'm on a mission, I gotta admit I love all that attention. A couple guys actually go so far as to grab my arm, but I just smile and continue to make my way toward my destination. I slide onto a barstool and ask the bartender for an appletini.

"Appletini, huh? Mmm. You've got great taste," says a dark-skinned chick sitting on the next stool over.

I nod my head and dismiss her quickly, because I'm not down with none of that lesbo shit.

I scan the crowd looking for my prey, but he's nowhere to be found. People are grinding on the floor, and some of them chicks are so naked you'd think it was summertime. I even notice a few in booty shorts and bikini tops. It's ridiculous, and if you ask me, they look like damn fools! *I guess ugly bitches gotta do what they gotta do to get attention. Not all of them hoes can turn heads like I can.*

A dude with unkempt dreads walks up to me and offers to buy me another drink, but I decline. By the looks of things, he can't even afford a damn appletini. His dingy white tee, faded-ass Levi's, and white Air Force 1s ain't the business, and they've all seen better days. Too dumb to take the hint, he still slides his dusty ass onto the barstool beside me and tries to spark up a conversation.

I ignore him, but he doesn't take heed that I don't wanna be bothered, and he's beginning to irritate the hell outta me. Trying to remain calm, I spin the barstool around till my back is to him, but he continues to talk.

"Hey, girl. Mike's on his way over here. He had to park down the street," I hear from the dark-skinned girl who came on to me earlier. She casts me a sly grin, letting me know what's up.

Peeping game, I play along, hoping it will get the damn bug-a-boo out my face. "Thanks, girl. I was wondering where he was."

Dread Head gets the point because he gets up from the barstool and goes on about his business.

"Thanks," I tell the chick, grateful for the escape route she made for me.

"No problem, girl. I get it all the time." She smiles. "By the way, I love those shoes." She nods down toward my zebra-print Manolo Blahnik cuff-ankle boots.

"Thanks. Yours are hot too."

"Thank you, but I don't even like these damn things. They ain't even my style." She moves her feet from under the barstool to give me a better look. "My man bought 'em for me just for this damn party, but I'm damn sure throwing these bitches in the back of the closet when I get home."

Cachet

I join her in a laugh, but in the back of my mind, I gotta wonder how much money her man's got that she can just throw a pair of Yves Saint Laurent's in the closet. I know those boots cost just under $1,500. Then again, I don't have to wonder long, because a minute later, my heart drops when Taz walks up and kisses her right on the lips.

He looks sexy as fuck in all black. The short-sleeved Ralph Lauren Black Label shirt hugs his chest just right, while the black straight-leg jeans reveal a bulge in his pants that makes my mouth water. On his feet are high-top leather Gucci sneakers, in black, of course, and he's wearing a matching interlocking G belt. He's not rocking much jewelry: only a platinum bolt-lock chain necklace and matching bracelet.

"Hey, boo. What you doin' ova here?" he asks, looking at her lovingly.

"Nothing. Just sitting here talking to…uh, I'm sorry. I been running my mouth all this time, and I didn't even ask your name. I'm Osha," she says, smiling at me.

"Brandy," I say. "My name is Brandy. Nice to meet you, Osha," I stutter, still in absolute shock that Taz is her man.

"It's nice to meet you too." She turns back to look at Taz. "Baby, I just been sitting here gabbing away to Brandy—you know, a little girl talk." She smiles. "I was telling her about these damn boots you wanted me to wear tonight," she says, lifting her leg to draw his attention to the shoes.

"Osha, you know you gotta be the center of attention up in this bitch. You representin' me, baby."

"I know, boo. That's why I wore them, even though I hate the damn things," she says with a giggle.

"A'ight. Well, look, I gotta go, but it was nice meeting you, Brandy."

They share a long, tongue-tangling kiss before he tells the bartender to put my drinks on his tab, whatever I want. Little does he know that what I want is his ass.

Osha and I sit at the bar and get to know each other a bit. I feed her just enough information to keep her talking, and believe me when I tell you, that girl can talk! I found out they have three children: a six-year-old son, Terrence Jr., and five-year-old twin girls, Trinity and Charity. After a while, Osha's so tipsy she starts telling me anything and everything. With her drunk, loose lips she explains that they live in a six-bedroom, four-and-a-half bathroom house on Stockbridge Road in Akron. I'm glad she's talkin', though, because I need to know as much as I can about Taz so I can come up with a Plan B, now that I know he's got a girl.

When the DJ plays "Get Busy" by Sean Paul, Osha just about loses her damn mind. She snatches me off the barstool so fast I almost twist my ankle. "Oh my God!" she yells. "I love this song!" she shrieks over the music while pulling me through the crowd by my hand.

The floor is bananas! Bitches and niggas are everywhere, bumping and grinding all over the place. Osha stops in the middle of the floor and starts to dance; I gotta admit the girls got skills. I initially had no plans to shake what my mama gave me, but when I see Taz walking toward us, that changes in a hurry. In tow is some tall, light-skinned dude who's got money pinned to his shirt, so I assume he's gotta be the birthday boy.

To his left is Zema, smiling and grinning like she just won the lottery or some shit. "I'm happy you made it!" my hairstylist yells in my ear as soon as they get close enough.

I smile and give her a fake hug.

"This is Dan, my boyfriend," she introduces. "Dan, this is

my girl, Brandy."

He licks his lips and smiles, revealing the most perfect set of teeth I've ever seen—so white that he must have stock in Crest Whitestrips. I've gotta give Zema credit, because her dude is a cutie. He's about five-nine, with a slim but toned body. His goatee starts at his sideburns, and I can tell he's got good hair, because waves like that don't come from brushing. He looks as if he's got a little bit of cash, but clearly his money ain't as long as Taz's. You'd think that since it's his birthday, he'd be rocking one of the best outfits in here, but that's definitely not the case. Sure, he looks nice, but the ensemble he's wearing doesn't exactly scream, *"It's my birthday, and I'm a baller."* The dark-washed jeans match the jockey on his beige and blue Ralph Lauren shirt to the tee, and the butter Timberlands complete the look. As far as bling, he's got a small diamond stud in each ear, along with a platinum dog tag with small diamonds throughout.

"Nice to meet you, Brandy," Dan says, reaching for my hand.

I place my hand in his to shake it but pull it away when I feel him caressing my hand with his thumb. *Shit! Men can be so disrespectful.*

Zema don't even notice her man flirting with me. Instead she yells, "Hey, boo!" to Osha before they embrace. I figured they were best friends, especially since their dudes are best buds.

"Dance, Brandy, girl!" I hear Osha shout as she and Zema do they thing.

Taz and Dan are watching us, so I decide it's as a perfect time as ever to catch his eye.

"Yo, sexy ladies want par with us..."

I do a quick two-step and work my way to the ground,

running my hands over my body as I move to the beat. I stand back up and turn around, real sexy like, then grind on nothing but the air, all the while looking Taz directly in his eyes. He doesn't break contact, and I neither do I.

Yo, shake that thing Miss Kana Kana shake that thing. Yo, Annabella shake that thing…".

I bend forward, touching my ankles with my hands and pop and jiggle my ass like there's an earthquake in my pants. The crowd forming around me only motivates me to dance harder. Osha and Zema are dancing beside me, but they're no match for me and my ass-popping skills. I start to get hot—in more ways than one—so I take off my jacket and place it under my left arm.

The DJ stays with the Sean Paul theme and mixes in his cut with *Beyoncé' called Baby Boy.*

"Ah, oh my baby stop baby go. Yes, no hurt me so good baby oh…"

I lip-synch to the music in the middle of the floor as I make love to myself. My mind is clear, and my eyes are closed as I allow the music to guide my body. The belly-dancing skills I acquired back in the day allow me to seductively roll my stomach and hips to the mesmerizing beat. My head sways from side to side, and I start to feel myself to the fullest. I know damn well how sexy I am!

When I finally open my eyes, I see Taz and Dan staring at me like all the other niggas in the proximity, with lust in their eyes. Osha yells that she has to go to the bathroom, and Zema follows. That's cool with me, 'cause all I wanna do is stay on the dance floor and continue fantasizing about fucking Taz long and hard.

I can tell he wants me, so I make my way over to him and

start to dance, slithering my body all around, swaying my hips as I look hungrily up at his six-foot frame.

Picture us dancing real close in a dark, dark corner of a basement party. Every time I close my eyes, it's like everyone left but you and me..."

I slowly trace my lips with my wet tongue, careful not to smear my MAC lip gloss, then turn my back to him. When *Beyoncé* yells during the chorus, I grab hold of each leg of his jeans and pull him close so I can grind my ass right up against his manhood; I want him to feel exactly what it is I'm so willing to give. I drop down to the floor, then pick my ass up gradually so it rubs his dick along the way. He does nothing to stop me, and that alone lets me know I could have him tonight if I want him. As enticing as he is, though, a quick fuck ain't what I'm after. I stand up and turn around before walking away, leaving him wanting more.

About an hour later, the lights come on, and it's time to go. Osha and Zema return from their second bathroom break, and I thank Zema for inviting me, then let them know I'm about to bounce. They inform me that they're also about to leave and tell me to wait so they can walk me to my car.

"Nice ride!" Osha says once we're outside and in front of my truck.

"Thanks, girl. By the way, I had a blast tonight. We gotta hook up sometime soon," I tell her, fake as fuck.

"Yeah, that's cool. Give me your number, and I'll call you. We can do lunch or something."

I call out my number, then climb into my truck as they walk away. As I drive down the street, I see Taz holding the door of his silver Cadillac Escalade for Osha. After he closes the door, our eyes meet while I slowly drive by, and he smiles and licks his lips.

Mission accomplished! I knew all I had to do was run into that fine muthafucka and he'd be all up on me. Now all I gotta do is figure out how to get rid of Osha's ass. The poor girl don't even have a clue that she just befriended her new worst enemy, because I ain't gonna stop at nothing to get Taz right where I want him.

CHAPTER 4

It's the middle of February, and while I hate Walmart with a passion, I've gotta stop in there now and then to pick up a few things. I haven't been doing much in the past three weeks but sitting in the house, leaving only to maintain my hair and nails. I haven't seen Taz since the night of Dan's birthday party. He, Osha, and their kids have been in Florida for the past two weeks, but she's managed to stay in contact with me by phone. It plays perfectly into my plan; as soon as they get back from the Sunshine State, I'ma find a reason to take my hot ass to her house. What, you thought I was bullshitting? Hell naw! Taz is mines. Just gimme a little bit of time to prove it to you—and to him!

"Stop Ty'von!" a frail-looking woman yelled at a kid who looked to be six. He keeps knocking the candy off the rack, spilling Junior Mints and Reese's Cups all over the linoleum.

I do a double-take, because her face is way too small for her huge nose. She kind of resembles one of those troll dolls, only instead of that long, crazy hair, hers is extremely short and blonde, completely damaged and fried.

"Ty'von, I said stop!" she yells again when the boy launches a package of Skittles into the next aisle, not paying her ass a bit of attention.

The cashier stares at the child like she wants to pull her belt from beneath her ugly blue smock and beat his ass herself, but she continues to ring up the woman's items.

"I want a Snickers!" the little boy yells, then bends down and grabs one and opens it. As soon as he has the wrapper off, he takes a huge bite and stands there eating it like it's been paid for or some shit.

This causes two more children, probably four or five and presumably his bratty brother and sister, to do the same, and the other three in the cart—droopy-diapered toddlers—start screaming for candy too. The mother don't say another word and instead acts like she doesn't see a thing. She's wearing thick, ugly bifocals, so I'm sure she's blind as a bat, but that ain't got shit to do with her hearing! Everybody within range just looks at the bitch like she's crazy, wondering why she's not doing anything to stop them—and probably wondering if she ain't ever heard of birth control.

Suddenly, a light bulb goes off in my head, and I realize the situation might be beneficial to me. I'm about to come up off this ho, 'cause I know she's not smart enough to stop me, and I quickly put a plan into motion. "Are these your kids?" I ask politely.

"Yes, all six of 'em. Why?" she snaps, placing her hand on her bony-ass hip.

I've gotta catch myself before I tell the ho what I really feel. I compose myself and lie through my teeth, "I was just asking because they're so cute." There really ain't nothing cute about those little ugly, thievin' muthafuckas, and I'm sure she knows it. They've all got nappy-ass hair that they clearly inherited from their mama, and the three youngest in the cart are filthy, with crusty green snot dried on their faces. Still, my false compliment seems to have worked, because her smart attitude is gone when she speaks to me again.

"Uh…thanks," she remarks, as if no one has ever complimented her on her kids before, which is completely understandable.

By now, the brats have created a pile of wrappers and half-eaten candy on the floor, and one of them is throwing Lifesavers at the cashier.

"Ma'am, who's gonna pay for all this candy?" asks a frustrated store manager, a young white guy, looking at the mess they've made. Even though he only works at Walmart, he clearly took time to press his bright white shirt and tie, because there's not a wrinkle anywhere on him.

The woman looks down in her big, gaudy, ugly purse. "I don't got no money! All I got on my food stamp card is $23, and I've gotta buy my babies' cereal and milk with that," she says, gesturing toward the few groceries on the conveyer belt, just three boxes of Cocoa Pebbles and two gallons of milk. "If you expect me to pay for that candy, mister, I don't know what to tell you!" she yells, and I can't believe she has the nerve to get smart when her brats probably gobbled up and destroyed fifty bucks' worth of candy.

"I don't know either, ma'am, but you're gonna have to figure out something, because this candy isn't free," the manager exclaims, pointing at the wrappers and smeared chocolate. I can tell she's getting on his nerves, because his face and neck are beet red.

She raises her voice a couple octaves and says, "I guess you gon' hafta take it outta my ass then, 'cause like I said, I ain't got no fucking money!"

"Let me pay for it," I volunteer before the scene escalades into something even uglier. I had the manager a $50 bill and tell him to keep the change.

As I'm finally outside, walking to my truck, the frazzled blonde stops me. "Thank you so much," she says. "I don't know what I woulda done if you hadn't—"

I hold up my hand to stop her. "It's no problem, girl. My sister has to go through the same stuff all the time with her kids. I miss them so much," I lie with a straight face. As the words leave my mouth, I know I've got her—hook, line, and sinker.

"If ya don't mind my asking, how many kids does she have, and where are they?"

"She's got seven and one on the way. They live in Chicago now, but I know how it is. I love kids though," I lie again.

"Yeah, me too, even though they're a fucking handful!" She giggles and rolls her eyes.

No sooner do the words leave his mama's mouth before that holy terror Ty'von runs right out in the middle of the parking and almost gets himself hit by a blue Oldsmobile in dire need of a new muffler.

She runs after him and drags him back by the sleeve of his coat. "Girl, they might get on my damn nerves sometimes, but they're still my babies."

Yeah fucking right! I think in the back of my mind, but I'm not about to say that. "Yeah, I can see you love your kids," I say.

"I sure do, girl, especially since they daddies don't come around and do shit. I've gotta do all of it by my damn self."

"Daddies? I thought they all had the same dad, because they all look alike."

"Nope. All six of them each got they own daddy. There ain't no mistakin' their mama though, 'cause they all look like me." She laughs.

I don't crack a smile because I think it's sad. Not only do she got six babies by six different daddies, but every one of them little rugrats is cursed with their mama's horrendous looks and that nappy hair. "Well, look, I gotta go, but take my number and call me if you need anything." I scribble my number on the back of the candy receipt and hand it to her.

"Uh…all right," she utters in shock, looking like she doesn't know what else to say.

"I'm serious. My name is Brandy. Call me if you need *anything*. You remind me so much of my little sister, and I'd be happy to help out if I can," I tell her with a warm smile. "I know things gotta be hard for you with all them little ones all by yourself."

"Well, thanks again."

I walk away laughing to myself; without a doubt, that bitch will be calling me within the next two days. As I pull off, I see her piling her kids into a raggedy-ass gray minivan, and the same little bad-ass fights his mother tooth and nail as she tries to buckle his seatbelt. She pops him once upside the head, but not even that stops the little crazed bastard from flailing and carrying on. When she gets tired of playing, she hauls off and punches the kid directly in his chest, and I figure she knocked the air out of him 'cause it takes a minute before he can even scream from the pain. I have to laugh though. I can't blame the woman, because that little Ty'von is bad as hell!

Back at home, I put my few groceries away, then head into my bedroom. Before I even get a chance to sit down, my cell phone rings. I jump up to grab it, but it's not on the nightstand.

I run around like a chicken with its head cut off, but it stops ringing before I can find the damn thing. I pick up the cordless and dial my own cell number. I hear it ringing faintly, but I still can't pinpoint exactly where it is until I move closer to the closet. I shake my head when I remember dropping it in the pocket of my Ralph Lauren tweed coat that I had on earlier at the store. I dig it out of the coat, then scroll through the missed calls. When I don't recognize the number of the last call before mine, I call it back to see who it was.

"Hello?" a woman says somewhat shyly.

I hear all her loud-ass, mouthy, whining kids in the background and instantly know it's ol' girl from Walmart, but I act like I don't got a clue. "Somebody there just called my number."

"Yeah, this Sade."

"Who?" I ask, playing dumb.

"Is this…Brandy?" she asks impatiently.

"Yeah. This her. Why?"

"Um, I'm the girl you met at Walmart earlier today, the one with the crazy-ass kids." She laughs. "I'm sure you remember us."

"Yeah. What's up?" I knew she was gonna call me soon, but I damn sure didn't think it'd be an hour later. I figured she'd at least give it a day, especially since I already forked out fifty bucks for her kids' mess.

"Nothing, girl. What you doing?"

I suppress a giggle. I know she don't care about what I'm doing and that she's only trying to make small talk, distracting herself from her miserable life and those brats of hers. "Uh, I ain't doing much. Just got in, as a matter of fact, and I'm about to sit on the couch and watch some reruns of *Martin*. What them babies doin'?" I ask, as if I care.

She chuckles nervously. "Being bad as hell, as always." There's a slight pause before she continues. "Uh, I feel funny asking this since we just met and all, but you said to call you if I need anything, and…well, uh…"

"What you need?" I asked, just wanting her to spit it out so I can get off the phone.

"I was wonderin' if I could borrow some money, just so I can get my babies some boots and coats. I'll pay you back as soon as I get my check. It's just that it's so cold outside, and the worn-out li'l jackets they got don't fit and ain't thick enough, so—"

"Girl, don't even worry about it. I'll be happy to buy them some winter stuff. Can't have them freezing their little selves to death, can we?" I say, cutting off her rambling, though I know there ain't no way in hell she'll ever pay me back with her broke ass. "Gimme their sizes, and I'll go to the mall and pick out some things for them, then drop it off at your house tomorrow. Hold on a sec." I put the phone down so I can get something to write with.

She gives me the info on all six kids, and then I happily disconnect the call. It's not that I wanna go shopping for boots, clothes, and coats for her little brats, but I gotta make her comfortable with me before I ask her to do what I need her to do.

It's getting late, so I enjoy a hot bath and a glass of Moscato and call it a night.

* * *

2000…

Shoes that are two sizes too small hurt my feet as I walk the few blocks from school to our apartment. There are bumps on the front, and they are wearing thin—so thin that it looks as

Cachet

if one of my toes might pop out at any given moment. They seem to get tighter and tighter with every step I take, giving me blisters, and I curse my mother for forcing me to wear them. If she would stop spending all the money I make on dope, I could have new shoes, or at least some secondhand ones that actually fit. When my apartment comes into view, I quicken my pace so I can get to it faster and get my feet the hell out of those torturous shoes.

The minute I step inside, I kick the shoes off my feet as fast as I can and wiggle my toes free from the cramp that's been forming in them. After I toss them into the closet, I head to the bathroom to relieve myself. I unbutton the jeans that are squeezing the life out of the small bump I call a stomach.

No sooner than I sit on the toilet, the door bursts open, and in walks my mother. "Hurry yo' ass outta here, because James'll be up in a minute. He been asking about yo' ass all day. If you wouldn't have been wastin' yo' damn time at school, I'da had my money already," she says.

James is one of my regulars, a middle-aged man who's got a wife and children at home. He's a maintenance man for the apartment complex we live in, and he usually stops by my house about three or four times a week. Our sessions don't really last long, because most of the time, all he wants is some oral sex. When he wants to penetrate me, it don't last much longer, because he sure doesn't have much stamina. Even though he's gotta be some sick kinda bastard to wanna have sex with a eleven-year-old, I'm sorta drawn to James, and I bet he's a good daddy to his kids, 'cause when he gives me the money for my mother, he always adds a few dollars extra so I can eat. In a weird way, I'm grateful to him. So far, he's the only person who's ever shown me any love around here. I know my damn mama oughtta be feedin' me, but I'm quickly learning that if I wanna eat, I'm gonna have to sing for my supper, if ya know what I mean.

Still sittin' on the toilet, I answer, "Okay, Ma." That's all I can say, or she'll bust me in the mouth—or worse. As soon as she walks out and closes the door, though, I lower my head and sigh. I'm so tired of this shit.

I've been sleeping with the men she brings to the house for the past four years. She don't even have to have sex with them anymore, 'cause they only want me. I've slept with more men than I can count, and the numbers continue to add up. I used to cry about it daily, but I've gotten used to it, I guess, and I've learned to deal with it. When they're on top of me, I just lie there and allow my mind to take me to a better place—a place where I can be a normal eleven-year-old whose mama isn't also her pimp.

As soon as I exit the bathroom, a knock comes at the door. Assuming it's James, I walk over to look out the peephole that no longer has the glass in it. When I seem him standing there, I open the door and greet him politely before inviting him in. I figure he just got off work, because he's dressed in blue overalls and a ball cap and black work boots.

"Have a seat on the couch, and I'll be right back," I say, then hurry to my room and change out of my jeans and shirt into a nightie.

By the time I come out, James is already half-naked—the only half that really matters for me to earn my dinner.

After he's done, which doesn't take long, I get up and go into the bathroom and hop in the shower. I turn off the water and realize James is still here. I listen at the bathroom door to hear what he's sayin' to my mama, and his words nearly stop my young heart.

"Sophia, I'm telling you, that girl a yers is pregnant."

"Shut the fuck up, James! She too young to be fuckin' pregnant! She ain't even had a period yet, so it's impossible for her to be carrying a man's child!" she yells.

"I had a lotta pussy in my life, Sophia, so believe me when I tell you that Brandy's gone and got herself knocked up. Shit, you can look at her stomach and see that she's pregnant," he argues.

"Brandy! Get yo' muthafuckin' ass out here!"

"Just a minute, Mama. I'm not dressed yet," I tell her as I reach for my nightshirt and underwear.

"I don't give a fuck if your dressed or not. Everybody done seen yo' naked ho ass already. Get the fuck out here now!" she yells.

I move as quickly as I can. "Yes, Mama," I respond meekly as I take baby steps out of the bathroom. You'd think that since I've been selling my body for years, I wouldn't be shy about standing there in nothing but a towel, but I am.

"Have you had a period yet?" she asks, staring hard at me.

"Yes. I've had them since last year," I tell her, scared of what's going to happen next. I already know I'm pregnant, but I've been too afraid to tell her, and I'm not exactly happy that James has blown my dirty little secret.

Mama looks me up and down, and when her eyes land on the baby bump on my stomach, she explodes. "Bitch, are you fucking crazy? Who the fuck is the baby-daddy? Tell me, Brandy! You'd better tell me right fucking now!" she demands, rushing toward me like she's gonna beat my ass.

I throw my hands up to block the hits that I know are coming my way, but my effort to defend myself only angers her more. She must think I'm trying to fight back, because she starts screaming and yelling, reminding me I ain't too old to have my trifling ass kicked. She throws a shot that hits me square in the temple, causing me to fall to the ground. My head is spinning, and I ball up in an attempt to cover my midsection, but the way she's kicking and punching me makes it very hard to protect my body. I can't do anything but allow it to happen.

James finally pulls the furious woman off me, screaming for her to stop.

As soon as he helps me off the ground, I run back into the bathroom and lock the door behind me. I throw on my nightshirt and huddle beside the toilet bowl, praying that she'll just leave me alone. I try to think of what I've done to deserve this, and I wonder why she can't just love me like a mother is supposed to love her child.

"Come outta that fuckin' bathroom, you li'l bitch! I'm gonna kill you!" Mama yells as she kicks and bangs on the thin, rickety old door. I'm surprised the cheap-ass hinges hold, because every time she hits it, the door seems as if it's going to fall in.

I'm scared to open the door, but I'm also scared not to. "Mama, I'm sorry!" I cry out, hoping that, just this once, she'll feel sorry for me.

She doesn't, though, and she makes that clear when she calls me every name in the book and a few that I think she made up.

I sit on the cold, filthy, mildewy tile floor, scared and confused. I honestly don't know why she's mad at me, because all I've done was exactly what she told me to do. She makes me sleep with all those men; I ain't never had a choice. It's not like I went out and got pregnant by some neighborhood boy who promised to love me. I'm four months along already, about to have a baby at the age of eleven, and I ain't even got no clue who the daddy is.

Finally, the banging and threats stop, and I can hear James outside the door. "Come on out, Brandy. It's all right."

I step out slowly and look all around, but my mother is nowhere to be found. I don't know if she's in her room or where she went, and I honestly don't care, as long as she's not trying to kill me. Without another word, I just go into my room and shut the door, hoping to sleep off the throbbing in my head. Lying on top of my tattered sleeping bag, I drag my sheet up to my chin and somehow manage to drift off to sleep.

* * *

"Brandy, get out here!"

I jump when I hear my mother yell. I open my eyes and give them time to adjust to the darkness. My head is still hurting, and I'm freezing. I've got no clue how long I've been asleep, but when she calls my name again, I move as quickly as I can. The last thing I wanna do is tick her off again or get in any more trouble, so I follow my mother's voice into the living room.

I find her in there with James and a man I've never seen before. They are all surrounding a long metal table that's been placed in the center of the room. A perplexed look covers my face; I've got no idea what's going on, but something tells me it ain't gonna be good.

"Brandy, this man is here to help you," James says.

"What do you mean?" I ask, because unless he's here to take me away from the hell-hole I'm living in, he can't help me do nothing.

"He's a doctor, and he's gonna get rid of that bastard you've got growin' inside your stomach. Now bring yo' ass over here and let him do his job!" my mother roars.

I take a step back. She must be crazy in the head if she thinks I'm gonna let that man take my baby. It sounds crazy, but I'm actually looking forward to being a mother. Sure, it scared me at first, but in the past few months, I've grown attached to the little person I'm carrying in my womb. If I have a baby, there'll at least be one person in the world who loves me, and my child won't ever hurt me. That's all I've ever wanted—a person to love who'll love me back. I surely haven't gotten that from my mother or father; I've never even met him before, and if ya let my mother tell it, she's got no clue who he even is, so I guess that makes me a bastard too. A smile spreads across my face when I feel my baby move. A strange feeling comes over me, and I'm sure it realizes something isn't right about this situation.

Still facing them, I back up toward my bedroom door, hoping I can get in there, lock the door behind me, and climb out the window.

I'm literally an inch away when I feel James grab hold of me.

I kick and fight as he drags me toward that terrifying table. "Please stop! Let me go, James! Please!" I plead with tears in my eyes, but my desperate cries fall on deaf ears.

In no time, the doctor is there to give him a helping hand, and they both carry me over to the table and lay me on top of it against my will. I continue to fight, doing everything in my power to keep them from doing what they're trying to do, but it's of little use. With little effort, they stretch my arms apart and lock them into these leather restraints. My legs are still free, so I kick them violently, but they tie them down in no time.

The doctor takes a pair of scissors and cuts my nightshirt off, until I'm lying on the cold table, naked as the day I was born. He places his hand on my stomach and pushes gently with two of his thick fingers, then rubs it in a circular motion. "I'd say she's up there, 'bout four to five months," he diagnoses.

"Please, Mama, don't let him do this!" I cry out as the tears run slowly down the sides of my face, landing on the table.

"Just hurry up and get the little muthafucka out of there," she says coldly, ignoring me. "I can't stand a sneaky-ass bitch! How did she think she was gonna get this past me, like I wouldn't eventually find out?"

I feel a small amount of pressure before excruciating pain, and all I can do is scream. It feels as if he is constantly stabbing me with a knife, and I can't do anything about it, but lie there and allow it. I howl from deep in my soul. When my mother tires of hearing me scream, she walks over and shoves a dirty sock in my mouth, till it's hard for me to even breathe. I pray that God will kill me, because I can't take it anymore. Just when I'm about to pass out from the pain in my body and my heart, the doctor says he's done and unfastens the leather straps from my arms and legs. I attempt to get up off the table but fall flat on my face, and not one of them tries to help me.

My mom doesn't care the least bit about the blood or the pain I'm in. She only asks the doctor, "Are you sure it's not alive anymore?"

If I've ever felt any bit of love for her, that question just killed it for me.

* * *

Buzz! Buzz! Buzz!

I reach my arm over and hit the snooze button before pulling the covers over my head. My pillow is wet, and there are still fresh tears in my eyes. After five minutes of lying in bed, trying to shake the cold, cruel memories out of my head, I realize I really need to get up so I can make it to the mall before it gets crowded.

I stagger into the bathroom and turn on the shower. In minutes, the bathroom begins to get foggy from the hot water. I wipe the steamy film off the mirror so I can apply a fresh layer of AMBI to my face. Once that's done, I put my shower cap over my silk head scarf and climb into the shower stall.

The warm water feels good against my skin, and I stand in one spot, savoring the moment. I pour some of my David Yurman shower gel into my loofah, then wash my body from my neck to my toes before rinsing the AMBI off my face. When I turn around to rinse off, the water tickles my breasts, and I instantly think of Taz. Before I know it, my hands are massaging my perky 36-Cs. I throw my head back and pinch my pointed chocolate nipples between my thumbs and fingers as the soothing water rains down on me. Keeping my left hand in place, I trace a path to my pubic hair with the right one and begin rocking my hips to a made-up beat. I split my pussy lips and thrust my middle finger into my tight pink hole. "Ahhhh!" I cry out. Two, then three fingers move inside me, and I thrust them in faster and faster. It's been a while since I've had some, and I'm enjoying every minute of it, even if I'm entertaining myself.

With my left hand, I feverishly work my clit in a circular motion while spreading my legs further apart. I can feel my nut building deep inside, and I at the moment, I desperately need it. My body trembles, my eyes are closed, and my mouth shapes in a wide O. *Just a few more strokes, and I'll be there.*

"Aw shit!" I shriek as I cum hard on my hand, so hard that my knees weaken, and I have to catch myself on the towel rack.

I pull myself up just enough to turn shower off before succumbing and just lying on the wet shower floor until I can come down off my nut. Once my breathing normalizes, I bring my hand to my mouth and lick every finger clean, savoring the taste of my juices. I can see why Roger used to love to eat my pussy, because it tastes like honey.

Following my freaky session with myself, I finally get up enough energy to get dressed and head out of the house. My destination is Parma Town Mall, where I'll pick up a few nice things for those undeserving kids. I don't think it'll be too hard, considering her kids are stair steps, and I can buy them all pretty much the same things.

Two hours and $1,500 later, I'm on my way to Sade's house. I ain't even trippin' about the cost, because as far as I'm concerned, it's money well spent—an investment, if you will. In the end, I'll make way more than that off ol' girl when I get her to do me this one favor.

When I turn onto Lomond Boulevard to find the address she gave me, I'm shocked to see she lives in a fairly decent neighborhood. I pull up to her house and am floored; the place is beautiful. I check the address I wrote down, just to make sure I'm at the right place, as I'm sure my GPS has done some screwed-up shit and told me wrong. Then I see the same old gray, beat-up-ass minivan she was driving at Walmart, and I know for sure I'm where I need to be. I pull my truck to the driveway of the two-story, all-brick house, then get out and walk up to the door.

"Who is it?" I hear after I ring the bell.

"Brandy."

"Hey, Brandy!" she says as soon as she opens the door, probably shocked that I actually came through for her.

"Hey, girl. I got some bags in the car for you."

"Okay. I'll help you."

We bring everything into the house and set it down on the dining room table.

"Please stay for a minute," she says, motioning to places where I can sit.

I take a seat in one of the chairs. I'm afraid to sit down anywhere else because the house is so damn nasty! There are cereal bowls on the floor, full of curdled milk that looks like cottage cheese. Toys and bags of dirty, smelly clothes are everywhere, and I have to wonder, *How in the hell did a sloppy-ass bitch like this get a place this nice?* "I love your house, girl," I say, hoping it will bait her enough to start talking.

"Thanks, but I really gotta clean up."

No shit.

"The kids were a little wild today."

Muthafuckin' liar! There ain't no way in hell all this filth happened in one day. Nasty bitches kill me when they say dumb shit like that! "Where you work, girl? I know the rent gotta be high as hell out here in Shaker," I ask.

"Shit, I can't afford no babysitters so I can work. I got Section 8. They pay all my rent in this big-ass five-bedroom house. You want me to give you a tour?"

"Naw, maybe next time. I got someplace I gotta be today, but I just wanted to swing by and drop off the kids' clothes," I lie. I ain't about to walk through this nasty muthafucka. Ain't no telling what the rest of the house looks like. I don't wanna fuck around and get my nice shoes stuck in one of those sticky patches on the rug or something. "Where them babies at anyway?"

"They bad asses taking a nap. They should be up any minute."

Naptime, huh? Good. That's my cue to get the hell outta this house. They were acting like damn fools at Walmart, and I'm sure they aren't any better at home. "Well, I got them about ten outfits apiece from The Children's Place. They all got Timberlands and Polo coats, with the matching hat and gloves," I say as I stand up and make my way toward the door. "Call me if you need anything else, girl."

"Thank you so much, Brandy! No one has ever done anything like this for me before, and I am extremely grateful," she tells me with tears in her eyes.

"No problem. I'm happy to help however I can. Oh...I forgot to give you these," I say, handing the receipts to her. "Just in case you have to return something."

"Oh my God! You spent $1,500?" she shrieks.

"Yeah, but it ain't nothing. I told you I got you. Call me later."

"Okay," is all I hear as I close the front door and head to my car.

I smile as I pull off, happy that I've set the wheels in motion. *I bet she thinks I'm an angel sent from above, but she couldn't be more wrong!*

CHAPTER 5

It's April, and spring is in full effect. After Osha and Taz got back from Florida, we started spending a lot of time together, just like I planned. She's actually started to think of me as one of her best friends. For the past two months, we've been shopping and clubbing a lot, and sometimes we just chill at the house. I'm not mad, because it's all part of my plan. I'm just workin' toward my goal; little does she know that my goal is to get my hands on her man. Sure, Taz wants to fuck me, but he loves the shit outta Osha, and I know he won't leave her unless she does something foolish, so I've gotta stick around till I figure out how to turn her into a fool.

It's supposed to be in the eighties today, and they invited me to a cookout at their house, a small get-together for Osha's little sister, Asha. It's sort of a combination birthday/graduation party, since Asha will be heading off to college in June. I wanna look cute but comfortable, so I put on a white and black polka dot Versace dress with the black lace belt around the waist that looks great against my mahogany skin. I also throw on my black Alexander Wang patent-leather wedges. I pull most of my hair into a tight bun, with the exception of my bangs, which fall just below my eyebrows. I look in the mirror and wink at myself, admiring the black and white three-carat heart-shaped earrings. The matching necklace, bracelet, and ring complete my outfit. The last thing I need to do is transfer the items from the purse I wore yesterday into my patent-leather Valentino hobo, and I'll be ready to roll.

As soon as I pull up and park behind Taz's red Dodge Viper, my panties instantly get wet. *Mmm. This bitch is prettier than a muthafucka. I can just picture myself deep-throating the hell outta Taz's dick while he whips this bitch in and out of traffic.* I shake the naughty thoughts from my mind, put on my bestie hat, and make my way toward the house.

Since I've got an open invitation, I walk right into the unlocked door of the huge two-story brick house. From my place in the foyer, I see Osha in the kitchen, stirring something on the stove.

Before I get there, Trinity runs up to me and hugs my legs tightly with her little arms. I'm not usually one to deal with kids, but she and Charity are an exception. If I ever had children of my own, I'd want them to be as cute as those little divas. "Hey, Brandy! I missed you!" she tells me.

I smile at how cute she looks in her pink Polo dress and matching Polo canvas shoes. "Hey, Trinity! I've missed you to. Where's—"

I'm cut off when Charity bolts from around the corner and right into me. "Hey, Brandy!" she sings as she hugs me in the same spot Trinity did. She's wearing an identical outfit, only in lilac. If I can't say anything else about Osha, at least her kids are always fly. "Mommy's in the kitchen, and Daddy's grilling hotdogs outside on the grill." She smiles, showing the gap where her two front teeth used to be.

"All right. I'm about to go see your mommy real quick okay?" I ask before I turn to walk toward the kitchen.

"Okay," Trinity says. "Oh, and Brandy…"

"Yes, Trinity?" I turn around and look back at her.

"You're working that dress, girl!"

I burst out laughing. They say stuff like that all the time, and that's why I love these little girls. "Diva!" I yell from the kitchen, causing Osha to jump.

"Damn it, Brandy, you scared the shit out of me, girl," she says, giggling while holding her hand across the food-stained apron. Her huge breasts jiggle and bounce beneath it, and all I can do is shake my head. She only weighs about 110 pounds, so I've got no idea how she carries those big-ass jugs around without tipping over. "Yo' ass gotta be fly no matter where you go, huh?" she teases.

"Hell yeah! Never know if I'm gonna run into my next boo," I tell her, twirling around and causing my dress to balloon out. What she doesn't know is that my plans are to snatch up *her* boo, but only when the time is right.

If I wasn't plotting on her man or could trust a bitch farther than I can throw her, Osha might make a cool girlfriend. When I first met her at the club, I thought she was a lesbian tryin' ta spit game on me, but now I know better. She's really just a down-to-Earth, easy-to-talk-to chick. Best of all, since she has her own money, I never have to worry about her mooching off mine. The one thing I can't figure out is why Taz is so in love with her. Don't get me wrong: Osha is a beautiful girl. Her chocolate skin doesn't have a blemish on it, and she doesn't even need to wear makeup. Plus, I already mentioned those huge titties of hers. What gets me is that he's so flashy, while she's a plain Jane type who doesn't dress fly at all; she's more comfortable in jeans and a baby tee. Her hairstyle's never anything special, and she always wears it bone straight, hanging down with a part in the middle. Other than that big-ass chest, she doesn't have any other assets. Matter of fact, her ass is as flat as a deflated tire. Whatever it is that makes him love her so much, my plans are to put a stop to it.

"What's up, Brandy?" I hear over my shoulder.

I look up and see Asha standing over by the refrigerator with a bottle of water in her hand. "What's up, Mama? I didn't even see you over there. You ready for the college life?"

"Damn straight! I'm ready to get my party on!" she yells, throwing her hips from side to side and dancing to her own beat.

She's dressed adorably in a white, strapless romper and a pair of gold flip-flops. Her gold charm necklace matches her bracelet. She always looks cute and dresses way better than her sister Osha. Facially speaking, the two could be twins, but their built exactly the opposite from one another. While Osha has huge breasts, Asha's got none, and Asha's got ass for days to rival Osha's flat behind.

"You better not be doing too much damn partying, or Taz will kill you," Osha warns, rolling her eyes.

"Geesh! I'm just playing," she says before she turns to saunter away. "But I *am* gonna get my boogie on though!" she hollers over her shoulder before running into the back yard.

"That girl is crazy as hell," Osha says, shaking her head. "I'm serious. She best not get out there and start messin' up, or Taz'll have her ass."

"What you mean?" I ask.

"He's paying for her to go to school, so if she screws it up, he'll be pissed."

"Oh. I didn't know that. It's good of him to look out for your sister like that. What school is she going to again?"

"She was supposed to go to Cleveland State, but she got accept at Spellman, so she's going there to study art."

"That's what's up! I'm happy for her. Damn, I wish I woulda gone to college. I bet I'da had a blast."

"See? That's what I'm worried about."

We share a laugh, and then I keep Osha company for a while before I head outside to see what my future man is doing. The back yard is full of people, all dancing, talking, and swimming in the built-in Olympic-sized swimming pool. I wave to Zema, who is sitting on Dan's lap in one of the lounge chairs. She's wearing some sort of flowery dress, and from where I'm standing, it's ugly as hell. Terrence Jr., TJ, is standing at the top of the swimming pool slide, waving like crazy. I just laugh and wave back; it's funny how much that boy looks like his daddy.

"What you got on that grill for me?" I ask seductively.

Taz's back is to it me, and he's flipping burgers on the grill, so he replies without turning around, "Brandy, I've got whatever you want."

"Boy, you betta stop playing befo' you get me in trouble."

"You a grown-ass woman, Brandy. Can't nobody get you in trouble but you." He turns around, and we face each other.

I can't help inhaling a strong whiff of his Clive Christian No. 1 cologne; it's intoxicating, worth every bit of the $2,000 he spent on it. "I hear you, Taz, and you're absolutely right. Can't nobody get me in trouble but me."

"See? You learn something new every day. Now it's up to you to put it to good use." He winks before looking me in the eyes. The look clearly tells me that if he could lay me down and fuck me right here and now, he would.

Cachet

I just bite the corner of my bottom lip and giggle before I
turn to walk away.

As soon as I turn around, I see Zema giving me the evil
eye, staring at me like she knows what I'm up to. I stare right
back, then roll my eyes—my way of telling the bitch to mind
her fuckin' business. *Her man is sitting under her, and if
she's gonna show up in a horrid-ass dress like that, she best
worry about him and not what the fuck I'm doing.* She'd be
salty as fuck to know her man's always trying to pass me his
number every chance he gets. I decline not because of her,
'cause I couldn't care less about taking a nigga from a bitch,
but because he ain't got enough money for me. I wouldn't
even let his broke ass smell my pussy, let alone fuck me. He's
just Taz's follower, and he ain't got no real paper. I'm sure he's
playing the fuck outta her with other bitches, though, because
he looks just like Shemar Moore, and you know hoes love
that.

My phone rings, and I see that it's Sade. I've been dodging
her calls for the past month, but I answer it this time, when I've
got an excuse to get off the phone quick since I'm at the party,
hoping she'll finally leave me alone. "Hello?"

"Brandy? What's up? You got my money?" she inquires,
getting right to the point.

"What money? What you talking about?" I ask, playing
the fuck out of dumb. I know she wants her money, but I ain't
giving her a damn thing! That money is sitting pretty in my
back account, and she ain't got shit coming. That's what her
dumb ass gets for thinking she was gonna get over on me like
I'm stupid.

After I spent all that cash on those clothes for her bad-ass
little snot-nosed brats, she started calling me almost every

day, asking for more shit: money to get her van fixed and buy stuff for her house and even for tampons! What female asks another bitch for shit like that? She didn't have no shame, and I was starting to think she thought I was her man or some shit! I gave her everything she asked for without a problem, and I guess she thinks I'm some kind of dummy, because about a month later, I told her about this lick I had where she could get a tax refund even if she didn't work a day that year. I told her I could get her $5,000 for three of her kids if she let me claim the other three, and she accepted.

What I didn't tell her was that I'm the one who does the taxes. I got $7,500 a piece for us, and since she didn't have a bank account, I had to deposit it all in mine. About a week after I filed the tax paperwork, she called me and started talking like she didn't think it was fair that I got five grand off her kids, and that bitch had the audacity to ask me for half of my refund check! I told her I'd give it to her, but right from the jump, I knew I was lyin'; I ain't giving that bitch shit. She must be out of her rabbit-ass mind if she thinks I'm taking a short on my money. She didn't have a problem spending my shit when I was splurging on her and those troll-looking things she calls kids. It's been about a week since I got the money, and I have yet to give her one fucking dime.

"Where the hell is the money you promised me?" she yelled.

"First of all, calm down, 'cause I ain't the fuckin' one!"

"Girl, what the fuck ever. Do you got my money or not? If you don't, I'ma call the IRS and report you for tax fraud. I'll tell 'em I didn't give you permission to claim my kids, and that'll fuck yo' shit all up!" she threatens.

"Do whatever the fuck you want, 'cause it ain't even that serious," I bluff, thinking of a quick lie. "We got audited, and the feds put a hold on both our checks. I checked online, and it says we'll have to wait a month. Happy now, you impatient bitch?"

"Why didn't you just call and tell me that? I've been calling you for weeks."

"I ain't had no phone. My shit broke, and they took their damn time getting me a replacement. I ain't wanna pay they asses $500 for a new one, so I had to wait."

"Oh. Sorry, Brandy. I was worried you were just trying to get over on me. Just keep me posted okay?"

"Sure," I lie. After she hangs up, I get pissed all over again. *How dare she call me, talking all reckless, like I'm some sort of punk bitch or something? Shit! Now I gotta show her my real bitchy side, 'cause I don't play when it comes to threats. Yeah, I got somethin' for this ho', and it damn sure ain't money. When I give it to her, she gonna wish she never fucked with my candy-buyin' ass at Walmart that day.*

Back inside the house, I take a seat at the kitchen table with Osha, who's peeling potatoes for the potato salad and mixing the pie fillings. I watch her closely, and I wonder if I could ever be someone's wife. I doubt it, because you gotta trust somebody with your heart if you're gonna truly love and commit to them, and I don't think I'm capable of that. The last person I loved lied to me, and that shattered my fuckin' heart. After that, I promised myself I would never do that again. It's crazy, because it was two years ago, but I can still remember it like was yesterday...

***

2008...

I'm sitting on the couch when my landline rings, and a smile graces my face when I see "Roger Vines" on the caller

ID. He's been working in Florida for the past two weeks, and I've missed him so much. I can't wait to let him know I finished all my credits at LifeSkills and that I'll be graduating in July. We've been together almost two years, and I couldn't be happier. "Hey, baby!" I sing into the receiver.

"Sorry, bitch, but this ain't your baby!" a woman yells in my ear.

"Excuse me?" I ask, looking at the caller ID to make sure I read it correctly. The name is Roger Vines, but the phone number is one digit off.

"You heard me. I said this ain't your baby, bitch!" she yells again, angrier this time.

"Wh-who is this?"

"Mrs. Vines."

My heart drops into the pit of my stomach when I realize the awful truth: If there's a Mrs. Vines, Roger must be married.

"I want you to stay away from my husband. Naw, fuck that. You will stay away from my husband, or I'll take everything you've got, including that bullshit-ass car and that small-ass apartment that are in his name," she threatens.

Click.

After she hangs up, it takes a few minutes for the shock to wear off. Finally, I'm actually able to put my own phone back in its cradle. I'm sure this can't really be happening. Roger can't be married, because he promised me that I'm gonna be Mrs. Roger Vines! I just know somebody's gotta be playing with me, some lame-ass kinda prank. I pick up the phone and dial Roger's number.

He picks right up. "Hey, sweetheart."

"Are you married?" I ask, cutting right to the chase.

"Huh? Wh-what did you say?" he stammers.

Cachet

"If you can say huh, you can hear. Now, I'm gonna ask you one more time, Roger. Are you married?" Tears start spilling down my face, because I already know the answer. I also know he's gonna lie to me and try to deny the bitter truth.

"Who told you that?"

"Answer the fucking question, Roger!" I yell.

"Listen, baby, I love you so much. I swear I do. You just gotta believe me. You mean the world to me, and my life wouldn't be complete without you in it. Please just let me explain. I—"

"I asked you not to lie to me. I begged you, Roger! Why? Why would you do this to me?" Salty snot starts running from my nose, but I do nothing to stop it. My heart is hurt, I'm lost, and I don't know what the hell to do.

"Brandy, please just listen to me! I'll do anything to make this right. I just need you to listen. See, I was gonna tell you about her after my divorce goes through. I don't love her. It's you who I love. If you'll just give me a chance, I'll prove it to you." It sounds as if he's crying too, and he continues begging, "Just give me some time to book a flight, and I'll head over there the minute my plane lands so we can talk this thing out, baby."

"There's no need for that."

"All right. Do you just wanna talk now, on the phone?" he asks, sounding hopeful.

"There's nothing to talk about, Roger. You lied to me, and it's over."

"Aw, baby, please don't say that! Say anything but that! You can't mean it. I'll do anything you want. Just name it."

"What I want is for you to get the fuck out of my life and let me forget I ever met you."

"C'mon, Brandy! Baby, you can't mean that. You're just hurt right now, and that's understandable, but please don't do this. I love you. I really do. You gotta believe me. Give me a chance to—"

"Bye, Roger."

Click.

As soon as I hang up the phone, it instantly rings again. I take it off the hook and lie on the couch, crying and wondering why.

After a while, I stand and stagger to the bathroom to wash my face, but instead I fall to my knees and dry-heave into the toilet bowl. It hurts like hell, and there's nothing I can do but close my eyes until it's over. After that horrible episode, I wipe my mouth with the back of my hand and stand up. My back touches the door as I back out of the bathroom, and I slide down to the floor, crying once again. I wonder what is wrong with me and why nobody ever loves me the way they claim to or the way they should. I sit in that same spot for hours, crying until my body can't produce another salty, wet tear.

Finally, I jump up, suddenly pissed at myself for being so weak. I've got a plan, and I vow that this is the last time anybody's gonna fuck me over. I know how I'm gonna make Roger pay for what he's done to me, and I'm not gonna feel one damn bit of remorse for it.

I put the phone back in its cradle before I sit down at my computer to type an email to his sorry, lying ass:

Dear Roger,

I'm not even going to start off by cursing you out. I'm just going to get straight to the point. As you can see, I've attached one of the numerous videos I have of our sexcapades. I'm sure $500,000 would be enough to keep me from sending all my videos to your wife and the police station. See, last time I checked, it's still illegal to have sex with a minor, and you know damn well how young I am. You fucked me over and played games with me, and now it's my time to return the favor. I'll give you one week. If the money isn't in my bank account by then, I'll mail these videos to everyone you know, your wife and the police included. Please don't fuck with me, Roger, because I will not hesitate to do what I have to do. Your wife can have your sorry ass. I just want what's owed to me.

Have a nice life,
Brandy

Sending an email has never felt so good, and within ten minutes, he's calling my phone. I know he's pissed, but I don't give a shit; I know I've got the upper hand. "Hello?" I answer with attitude.

"What the fuck are you trying to pull, Brandy? Blackmail?" he asks loudly in my ear.

"All I want is what's owed to me, Roger, and nothing more," I state flatly.

"What the hell do you mean by that? In my book, I don't owe you shit. I've given your little ass everything you have now. Are you not satisfied with the apartment, the car, all those clothes I've bought you? What about your education? Are you telling me you aren't satisfied with how much I've already done for you? How can you say I owe you a damn dime when I've been—"

"Hell yeah you owe me more—a hell of a lot more,

Roger!" I scream, cutting him off.

"Come on now, Brandy. You know I love you, so why are we even talking about this?" He softens his voice. "I made a mistake, and I'm man enough to admit it, but you gotta believe I love you. I don't want to lose you. I just…can't."

"You love me?" I chuckle. "You don't love anybody but your damn self, Roger! I told you in the beginning how bad my life has been and how people have treated me, and boy did you take my sad-sack story and run with it! You know everything I've been through, and I thought…well, I really thought you were different, but you aren't." Apparently, my well of tears is restocked, because I begin to cry again. "I trusted you, you son-of-a-bitch, and you lied to me! I want my money by the end of this week, or I promise that you'll be sorry."

"What do I need to do to fix this, Brandy? There's gotta be something I can do to keep you from leaving me like this," he asked, totally disregarding my threat, which really was a promise.

"All you can do now is get me my muthafuckin' money!" I shout and slam the phone back in its cradle.

Just as I suspected, by the end of the week, my bank account is $500,000 richer. As soon as his check clears, I head down to the bank and withdraw every cent and deposit it in a different account so his triflin' ass can't find it. A few days later, I walk into a different bank and use some fake employment papers to get a loan. With 100 percent financing, it's easy to buy the condo I want. I use those same falsified documents to purchase my new vehicle; that and a nice li'l piece of pussy gets me just the truck I want.

Yeah, Roger did what I asked him to, but I'm still not

satisfied. I decide to send the tapes out anyway, and in no time, the police bust his sorry ass for statutory rape.

On the day of the trial, I can tell his head is all fucked up when I walk into the courtroom and testify against him. I put on a hell of a show, playing the victim like I'm auditioning for a Hollywood blockbuster. The judge slaps him with a five-year sentence, and when he gets out, he'll have to register as a sex offender. Before he fucked me over, he was a well-known plastic surgeon, but now he'll never practice again.

* * *

Damn, I'm glad that fucker has another year to serve before he's even allowed to ask for parole, I think as Osha heaps up a huge plate of food for me to take home with me.

The barbecue was great, and I can honestly say I had a lot of fun. I head home with Taz on my mind and the aroma of leftovers wafting into my nostrils.

I rely on my thoughts of Taz's fine ass to finger-fuck myself till I pass out, high off my nut and the fact that he and his money stacks will all be mine soon enough.

CHAPTER 6

Tonight, I've got a date with a guy named Xavier. I met him at the gas station the other day, a real cutie who was respectful about asking for my number. I've got so much going on in my life that I almost turned him down, but as I stood there pumping gas, it reminded me that I've been in need of some dick for a while, so I programmed my number into his iPhone. We conversed for a few days before he finally asked me out, and I accepted, figuring it will be my perfect chance for a quick hit-and-run fuck.

I stand in front of my mirror and look over my chosen outfit for the night, then remove the curlers from the top of my head and comb my wrap out. He wouldn't disclose where he's taking me and only said I should wear something sexy and make sure I'm hungry. Xavier doesn't really strike me as the hood type, so I guess it's pretty safe to say we won't be hitting up the nearby Red Lobster for dinner.

He begged to pick me up from my apartment, but I don't fuck around when it comes to where I rest my head, and I wasn't about to tell any random muthafucka where I live. For all I know, fine or not, the nigga might be crazy. So, I'm

Cachet

meeting him in a downtown parking garage.

When I pull up, he's already there waiting on me, and I'm glad he's not running late. His checkered tan Armani sport shirt blends well with his dark pants and tan Salvatore Ferragamo loafers, and I can tell he's a man of taste. Before I can even grab my door handle, he reaches to open the door for me.

"Thanks," I say as I take his extended hand and step out.

"My pleasure," he says, bringing my hand to his lips.

His eyes buck when he gets a full view of me; apparently, the black, sequined, one-shoulder bandage dress was a great choice. I smirk because the look on his face is priceless! I purposely brush my ass up against him when I turn around to close my door, causing him to groan. He chuckles before walking me over to his black Infiniti G37 and holds the door open. I get in and secure my seatbelt as he climbs in, and then we're off to wherever he's taking me.

"You smell good. What are you wearing?" I ask.

He smiles, revealing a perfect set of teeth. "Believe it or not, it's called A Taste of Heaven." His goatee is shaped to perfection, with not a hair out of place, and his lineup is the same.

All I can do is squeeze my legs together tightly, because my pussy is jumping with anticipation. He keeps licking his lips, and I can't wait to feel them all over my clit tonight.

* * *

Dinner is wonderful, and I gotta give him a lot of points for taking me to Morton's Steakhouse. The double-cut filet mignon, sautéed garlic green beans, and steamed asparagus are right on point.

When the bill comes, over $200, I watch him closely to see

if he'll flinch, but it doesn't seem to faze him. This pleases me, as it means one of two things: Either it isn't his first time here, or spending that type of money isn't a problem. Either way, I'm fine with that.

Since there's a wine tour going on this week, we head over to Geneva, for a wine-tasting on the lake. I woulda never thought something like that could be so fun and exciting, but I find I'm really enjoying myself.

Back in the car, I notice that he's heading back to the parking garage. "Where are we going?" I ask, sitting up and looking over the dash.

"It's getting late. I figured I better get you back to your truck," he says.

"Getting late, huh? You got a curfew or something? Because I sure as hell don't."

He smiles. "Really? Well, what did you have in mind?" he asks, licking those sexy-ass lips again.

"Just drive, Xavier. I'll tell you where to turn."

"Lead the way, ma'am," he says and places his manicured hand on my thigh.

As soon as the hotel room door closes, he's all over me, but that's right where I want him. I push his back up against the door and proceed to unzip my dress. I reach for the clasp of my strapless La Perla bra, and it takes me all of two seconds to take it off. As it falls to the floor, the chilly air-conditioned draft hits my nipples, and they become harder than rocks. Tracing my lips with my tongue, I turn around and bend over directly in front of him and remove the matching thong before strutting over toward the bed. My steps are slow, with just enough bounce that my ass jiggles enticingly with every step.

"Damn, baby, you sexy as fuck," he says in a husky tone

when I lie back on the bed and spread my legs.

My black Christian Louboutin butterfly platform pumps are beside my head, one on each side, and I dip my finger into my pussy a few times before bringing it up to my lips.

"Let me do that for you."

My breath catches in my throat when I feel his tongue enter my love canal. He fucks me with his mouth as I squirm and attempt to pull my clit away from its grasp. I decide that eating pussy must be an art for him, and I can tell you with a straight face that I ain't never had it this good. I feel his arms wrap tightly around my thighs as he pulls me closer, till I can't even move.

"Ahhhh!" I scream, since there's nothing else I can do. *There should be a law against what he's doing to me...and if it was, his ass would get the electric chair!*

"Why you keep running?"

"I...can't...take...it! Oh my God! Please...help me," I pant.

"You want me to stop?"

"Yes...no...shit, I don't know!" I say, and we both laugh. "I'm cumming! Shit, I'm cumming already!" My legs start shaking, and I fill his mouth with pussy juice, squirting my honey-sweet, tasty liquids down his throat. I try to pull myself away from him, to no avail; the hold he has on me is unbreakable.

"You done, baby?" he asks.

"Yes. Please...stop," I reply, out of breath.

"Okay. I'll quit with this, but I ain't done entirely," he says before roughly flipping me over onto my stomach. I look back just in time to see him open the gold wrapper with his teeth, and roll it over his pole with precision. In no time, he's easing into me, little by little. It hurts a bit at first, but the pain slowly subsides as my body adjusts to his thick shaft.

"Ahhh…" I exhale. My back is to his chest, my head is turned, and my mouth is inches from his; I softly bite down on his lip.

"Aw, shit! You tight as fuck."

"Get this pussy! Get this pussy!" I yell.

Xavier grips my ass cheeks from the back and spreads them. He drills his member deeper into my walls as I moan and cry out in ecstasy. "Yo sexy ass love this dick, don't ya?" he questions as sweat drips from his face and onto my back. He licks a trail with his tongue from my back arch up to my shoulders, then kisses my neck gently. If I didn't know any better, I'd say this nigga is actually making love to me.

I don't respond to his question. Instead, I just continue to throw my ass back and take as much dick as I can. He's giving me some crazy amount of pleasure like I ain't never felt before, and I feel like I might pass out any minute. He's got me feeling delusional. My eyes roll into the back of my head, and I bite my bottom lip. *This nigga is fucking the shit outta me!* I wouldn't have thought it was possible just by looking at him, because he's all respectful and conservative—a real fucking gentleman. But when he dropped them jeans? Baby, let me tell ya, ol' boy fucks like a porn star that's been in the business for a minute.

Just when I don't think I can take it anymore, he pulls out and turns me over onto my back. He pushes both of my breasts together and starts to feast on them. I grab the back of his head and bring it up toward my mouth, and we kiss like there's no tomorrow. I'm not big on kissing, but something about him makes me want to. Instinctively, my hips grind on him as we continue to kiss, and I can feel my wetness drip down into the crack of my ass. Slowly he kisses down my neck, between my breasts, and down my stomach, only stopping to swirl his tongue inside my belly button. My diamond belly ring makes a slight clinging noise when he pulls it gently between his teeth. He sits up and gives no warning before he enters me again.

"Sssssshhh-shit!" I groan.

With each of his thrusts, I bring my hips up to meet his. My hands are roaming all over his chest, and I love the way it feels. I can tell he works out on the regular, because a body like that ain't something a man's born with. We move in unison, uniting our bodies as one as we fuck each other like there's no tomorrow. Changing the pace a bit, he places each of my legs into the bends of his elbows and starts to long stroke me. I grab two pillows off the bed and prop them behind me so I can see his dick glisten as it goes in and out, and what a pretty sight it is! Every time he takes it almost all the way out, I tighten my muscles and squeeze as he slides back in.

"Damn, baby. What you doin' to me?" he questions.

"The same thing you're doing to me. I'm...blowing... your...mind!" I tell him, squeezing his dick as tight as I can.

I can feel my pussy contracting, and I know I'm about to cum again. I reach behind him and grip his sweaty ass cheeks and pull him in deeper; I wanna feel him all the way up in my stomach. Each time his dick glides across my clit, it brings me closer and closer to my orgasm. We're in the Ritz-Carlton, but I'm fucking like a prostitute in the Super 8. I keep screaming, and he keeps pounding, until my toes curl and my body starts to convulse and I cum, hard as hell.

Seconds later, he starts to pump faster, letting me know he's right behind me. "Ahhhhh!" Xavier yells, just before he pulls out and snatches the condom off. He pumps his dick with his right hand, and his babies drain onto my stomach.

When he's done, I lie there looking him right in the eyes, rubbing it in like baby lotion.

"Where the hell you been all my life?" he asks, exhausted.

"Right up under your nose," I say, and now I've got plans to fuck his brains out for the rest of the night.

CHAPTER 7

Two weeks later…

"Ugh! Why the hell do I pay a cable bill when it ain't never shit on TV?"

I'm irritated as hell because I'm sitting in the house all by my lonesome, bored out of my mind. My hair and nails are done, so here I sit, looking good, stuck in this bitch with nowhere to go and nothing to do. Osha is laid up at home with the flu, and Xavier is in North Carolina visiting his family. I would go to the Beachwood Mall, but it ain't shit in there that I want, and all my closets are already full as hell.

"My chick bad, my chick 'hood, my chick do stuff that ya chick wish she could…"

"Hello?" I answer.

"Where's my money, Brandy?" the caller snaps.

What the hell? I have to temporarily pull my phone away from my ear and look at it, in disbelief that anybody would dare talk to me all hard like that without even saying hi. "Well, hello to yo' ass too, Sade."

"It's the end of the month, and you have yet to call," she says smartly. "I'm tired of having to call you and ask you about this. You act like I owe yo' ass something. I mean, you should be calling me."

"Girl it's the fucking twenty-eighth, and the end of the month ain't till the thirty-first. You know how the damn government is about dates and shit. If they said the end of the month, they meant the actual *end* of the month. What, you think I'm tryin'a play you or some shit?"

"Naw, it ain't about you trying to play me. It's just that I always have to call you. When you do find out shit, you don't even bother calling me to fill me in. What the fuck is that about, Brandy? Man, I let you claim *my* fuckin' kids, and you all but disappear on a bitch. You don't call and say shit! When I call yo' phone, you barely answer, and you always talking about wait. I've waited long enough!"

"First of all, calm down. It ain't that serious, Sade."

"Calm down? What the hell you mean, calm down? We talking thousands of dollars here, and last time I checked, my ass is still broke. We got in this shit together, and you need to be telling me something! I ain't driving around in no damn Mercedes like you, with all that money up in my bank account. We ova here struggling while you eating good."

"What the fuck you want me to do, break into the fucking IRS and steal the money?" I yell, tired of this ho' trying me. "I can't get the money no quicker than they're willing to give it to me, so you can stop yelling in my goddamn ear! I tried to hook yo' ass up, but I guess you can't do shit for ungrateful-ass muthafuckas! You wasn't hollerin' all this nonsense when I was spending all *my* money on you and yo' kids, was you? Hell naw, because that was benefiting you! Yes, I drive a muthafuckin' Mercedes, but that's 'cause I worked hard for it, and I'm not about to apologize for it just because you've made so many fucked-up decisions with yo' life, havin' babies with six different niggas when you can't even feed yo' damn self!" I wasn't planning on yelling at her, but this bitch has me pissed the fuck off. *Who the fuck is she to call me and count my money? I have a right mind to go over there and beat the brakes off her ass for even thinking about talking to me like that. She's trippin' for real.*

"What are you saying, Brandy? That my kids were bad decisions?" she questions.

"I ain't saying that. All I'm sayin' is that you best not try to count my money, because you don't know what I've been through myself. You acting like I'm gon' run away with yo' money or some shit. You my girl, and I wouldn't even play you like that," I say, softening up a bit.

"Look, my bad, all right? I'm just stressing something awful. These kids are driving me crazy, and I need to get out for some fresh air. It feels like the damn walls are literally closing in on me. I really need a babysitter, but I ain't got no money to pay nobody," she says, sounding defeated.

"How about I watch the kids while you go out and have yourself some fun?"

"No shit, Brandy? You'd really do that for me? I would love that! Let me call my cousin and let her know we finally gonna have a chance to kick it!" she exclaims excitedly and with a totally different attitude than the one she was giving me a minute ago.

"Okay. I'll be over there around 8 o'clock."

"Thank you, Brandy. This means a lot."

"No problem. I'll bring them something to eat," I tell her before we hang up. I know you're probably wondering what the hell I'm doing, but I've got a plan, and tonight is the night

I'm gonna put it in action. Sade thinks shit is sweet my way, but I'm about to show her that I ain't the bitch to fuck with. She's gonna pay for all that threatening and shit-talking she's been doing, 'cause I can't let nobody get away with that shit.

* * *

Around 7:30, I pull up to her house. When she opens the door, I nearly lose my lunch. I can't believe she had the audacity to even answer the door that way. *What the hell? This bitch must think she's sexy, but how the hell you gonna answer the door in your panties and bra? Especially when your body is as fucked up as hers.* Her bra is beige, but it looks as if it's supposed to be white; then again, she doesn't even need it with her flat-ass chest. Another thing, I don't understand how she can be less than 100 pounds with her gut looking the way it does. I mean, I know she has six kids and all, but her stomach is ugly as fuck! It resembles a sloppy-ass bowl of spaghetti and has a lot of extra skin all over it. Ew! I can't see how any nigga would wanna fuck that, but then again, some niggas are too thirsty for their own good. In her case, at least six of them were.

"Have a seat. I'm almost dressed," she says before turning around and running up the stairs. Her Walmart big-girl panties sag in the back, due to the fact that she has no ass, and the ballooned out things jiggle in the butt with every step she takes, like she's carrying a pile of shit back there. The kids are on the couch watching *SpongeBob*, so I take a seat at the dining room table, completely disgusted by their mother.

While I'm waiting, I go into the kitchen to turn the food on. There are dishes piled in the sink, and it looks as if she hasn't cleaned up in days. The stove is covered with pots and pans with food still stuck to them. The floor is sticky, and with every step that I take my shoes make a noise like I'm stepping on chewing gum or candy or something. From the dish rack, I grab the only clean pot I can see, then locate a cheap-ass manual can-opener and twist the hell out of it to get the cans open. Once I've got the food cooking on her nasty-ass stove, I place the misfit lid on the pot and head back into the dining room.

About ten minutes later, Sade finally makes her way down the stairs, and I literally have to stop myself before I laugh right in her face. Her hair is parted to one side and slicked down with a thick coat of gel. It's all wavy and shit, and she even had the nerve to make two swirly lines where the baby hair normally is. Her light blue jeans are even worse, faded and wrinkled as hell, like she just pulled them out of the dirty clothes hamper.

"I hope your kids like Beefaroni," I say.

"Girl, they love that stuff! Thanks," she says as she grabs a denim jacket that's just as horrible as the jeans and puts it on over some old-ass Baby Phat t-shirt.

Where the hell is she goin', lookin' like that? I wonder, and I can't come up with a damn answer where that ensemble and that jacked-up hairdo would be appropriate.

"Y'all behave for Miss Brandy, you hear me?"

"Yes, Mommy!" they all lie in unison.

"I'm sure I won't have any trouble out of them," I say, and I know it's true, because I won't put up with none of their bratty bullshit, and I'm a lot less patient than their fool mama.

"Thanks again, Brandy. I'll call you when I'm on my way home."

"Okay. Have a nice time," I say as she walks out the door, even though I wonder how she's going to manage that. She don't even have a damn cell phone, but maybe her cousin does.

A few seconds later, she reemerges through the doorway with a light-skinned girl. "This is Meka, my favorite cousin," she introduces, as if I give a damn.

I stand up, still being phony, and shake the chick's hand, all the while thinking about how much she looks like a boy. She's tall as shit and has freshly done cornrows in her hair, braided to the back.

Sade says her goodbyes again, then finally disappears out the door once more.

I remain seated till I hear her beat-up-ass van start with a clatter and pull out of the driveway. As soon as I'm sure they're gone, I pull a jar from my purse and walk back into the kitchen. I lift the oversized lid from the top of the pot and pour in most of the jar contents, then stir it thoroughly before adding a little salt and pepper and closing the lid again. I'm amazed to actually find six clean bowls in the filthy, greasy cupboard, and I scoot several piles of junk mail and overdue bills aside to lay the bowls out on the counter. After I fill a bowl for each of the little brats, I add a little more from my jar into each bowl, just for good measure.

Starved as they are, the heathens finish the bowls off like vultures and even ask for seconds, which I have no problem giving them. After that, I allow them to sit on the couch and watch cartoons. I actually don't have any trouble with any of them, and that's a good thing.

By the time Sade gets home at 2:30, the kids are all passed out between on the couch and the floor. She thanks me and again, and I head home.

* * *

The drive is short, and in no time I'm pulling up into my parking garage and riding the elevator to my floor. I can't take my clothes off fast enough; I feel like the filth of her house is all over me. Right before I step in the shower, though, I'm interrupted by my ringing cell phone. Even though I don't feel like talking, I hurry over to answer it.

"What are you doing?" he asks.

"Nothing. What's up?"

"Meet me in about an hour."

"Okay. See you in a minute."

As I stand in front of my mirror wrapping my hair, I glance at my flawless naked body. I'm five-six, 137 pounds, and slim but thick in all the places that count. My chocolate skin is blemish free, and all my features are a perfect fit and complement one another. I have an oval face, round, bright eyes, and a small, almost dainty nose. Turning slightly to the left, I observe my high cheek bones and pouty mouth. My full lips part with a self-satisfied smile; even my teeth are perfect. There ain't many bitches out there who can fuck with me. This I know!

A few hours later, I'm lying in bed watching *Married with Children*. I'm in the process of dozing off when my cell phone rings again. "Hello?" I whisper, looking beside me.

"Are you sleeping?"

"No. Why? What's up?" I ask, sitting up.

"Nothing. It's just that Taz isn't at home, and I've been calling him for the past few hours," Osha cries into the receiver.

I roll my eyes, because I'm really not in the mood to play Dr. Phil. "Calm down, Osha. He's probably just busy and can't get to the phone," I try to reassure her.

"Yeah, or maybe his ass is laid up with some bitch and he ain't trying to answer!"

I chuckle. *She's got a point.* "Don't worry, girl. I'm sure it's nothing. Just take your medicine and get better so we can go away and let him worry about you for a change."

"You're right." She coughs twice before continuing, "I'm thinking Vegas. What about you?"

"You know what they say about what happens in Vegas, girl! Sounds like a plan to me," I say, wheels already turning in my head.

"Thanks, Brandy."

"For what?"

"You're always there for me."

"Hey, that's what friends are for," I say before hitting the end key on the phone.

"What she say?" Taz asks, stretching beside me.

"She's wondering why yo' dumb ass ain't answering her phone calls. She said she's been calling you for hours and that you're probably with some bitch and can't get to your phone."

"Well she's wrong."

"She is?"

"Yeah. I'm not with just some bitch."

I smile. "Is that right?"

"Yeah."

"Then who you with?"

"My baby," he says, laughing, then grabs me when I attempt to hit him with a pillow.

"You play too damn much!" I tell him.

"Huh? I play too much?" he asks, confused.

"Your baby is at home waiting on you."

"If that's the case, why am I lying here with you?"

"That's easy. 'Cause you wanted some pussy, that's why."

"I can get pussy anywhere."

"Yeah, but you can only get *bomb* pussy here," I say cockily, pointing between my legs.

"You do have some bomb-ass pussy, but I'm here because I wanna be, Brandy." He places his finger under my chin and kisses me deeply.

I know I said I wasn't going to start fucking with Taz right away, but his sexy ass was quick to wear me down. He started calling me on the phone all the time and popping up in different places. I tried to hold out but just couldn't. That fucker is persistent! I ending up giving him a shot of the pussy almost two weeks ago, and he's been sprung ever since. We've been meeting from time to time at the downtown apartment. Of course I'm trying to keep Osha from finding out about us, but it's hard because the nigga just can't keep his hands off me, even when she's around. Osha and I are going on a girls' getaway soon, and I know he's gonna leave her ass real quick as soon as we get back. I don't know why bitches are so · quick to trust another female, but I guess she's about to learn firsthand.

I climb out of his bed and make my way into the kitchen for a snack. I smile at the jar of peaches in the fridge, then grab it and a fork and head back upstairs to the bedroom to enjoy them.

"Yo' stingy ass didn't bring me nothing?" Taz pouts.

"You want some?" I ask, sticking my fork into a slice of the juicy, sweet fruit.

He responds by opening his mouth like a baby bird. When I feed it to him, he starts chewing on that peach like he's never eaten anything before.

"You ain't gotta chew like that!" I yell, playfully slapping him on arm.

I continue to eat peaches, occasionally sharing them with Taz, until my cell phone rings again. Thinking it's Osha, I put my finger up to Taz before picking up. "Hello?"

"How's my favorite girl?"

I can't help but smile at the sound of Xavier's voice. "I'm good. How about you?" I say in my little girl voice.

"Thinking about you and wondering when I'm going to be able to see you again."

When he says that, I close my eyes and picture the last time we were together. The sex was amazing! "What do you have in mind?" I ask, opening my eyes.

By now, Taz is giving me a look that could kill, but he's not my man, so I continue to talk, not paying his nosy, jealous ass any mind.

"How 'bout I come get you tomorrow and we go horseback riding? I've wanted to do something like that for a while now. You down?"

"Ooh! I'd love to go horseback riding!" I squeal, exaggerating my enthusiasm for Xavier's sake and just to piss Taz off and let him know what he's missing out on.

"I thought so," Xavier said, clearly smiling through the phone.

"Look, I'm about to go to bed now. I'll call you tomorrow okay?"

"That's fine, baby. Goodnight."

"'Night," I say, and we disconnect the call.

Out of the corner of my eye, I see that Taz is still glaring at me. I just pick up my peaches and continue to eat them, keeping my eyes fixed on the TV.

"Who the fuck was that?" he finally asks.

"A friend. Why?"

"Nothing. I just wanna know who the corny nigga is who's asking you to go horseback riding."

"Hater," I say flatly, then close the peaches, set them on my nightstand, and lay my head on the pillow, laughing to myself over his jealousy. *Men are so predictable!* I can feel his eyes peering at me as I turn onto my side, but I don't give a damn. *He's got a lot of fuckin' nerve even getting jealous when he has a bitch at home!*

Before long, I'm snoring lightly, looking forward to my plans for tomorrow.

CHAPTER 8

2001…

It's been almost six months since they took my baby from
me, and my days haven't gotten any easier. Mama didn't
even give my body time to heal, because within a matter of
days—two, to be exact—men started coming in to have their
way with me at all hours of the night. I'm no longer myself.
I'm just a shell of who I used to be. I stopped going to school a
few weeks ago. Honestly, what's an education going to do for
me? My birthday recently passed, but nobody said so much as
"Happy birthday." All I got was, "Hurry up so you can get my
money."

*The weather finally warmed up, and I'm happy about
that, because it means I can trade my too-small tennis shoes
for a pair of flip-flops. They're too little also, and my heels
hang off the back, but even that beats the hell out of having
my toes bunched up. I get off my bedroom floor and slide my
feet into the dingy white dollar store flip-flops, then pat my
pocket to make sure the $10 is still there. When James came
over earlier, he gave me extra for something to eat. I didn't
tell Mama, of course. I plan to get a bite at the corner store,*

Cachet

'cause I'm tired of eating warm Vienna sausages. If it was up to her, I'd never eat a thing, and there've been plenty of nights when my stomach has hurt so bad that I couldn't sleep. All I could do was lie in the fetal position and cry, listening to my tummy rumble.

"Where the fuck you goin'?" my mother yells as I walk past her toward the door.

"To the store," I reply, in no mood to explain things to her or to hear her run her mouth. I grab the doorknob quickly, before she can stop me, and make my exit.

I make my way back from the store quickly, because I'm hungry and my stomach is growling something terrible. When I enter the house, I notice that my mother is asleep on the couch with an empty needle beside her; of course she's high again, off money I earned with my body. I hope she'll be out for a while, because I really don't feel like hearing her mouth today. I also don't want her to see all the things I bought from the store. I creep past her slowly and almost make it into my room, but then she yells.

"I know you heard me talking to you when you was walking the fuck outta here!"

"No I didn't."

"Lie to me again, bitch, and I'ma come over there and knock yo' ass out! Now, where the fuck did you just go?"

"I told you I was going to the store."

"First of all, you don't tell me shit. You ask! Second, how the hell you gonna go to the sto' if you ain't got no damn money?" she questions, slowly lifting herself up from the couch.

I know to choose my words carefully; if I say the wrong thing, she'll absolutely flip. "Uh, I found some change in my room the other day, and I went to the store to buy something *to eat."*

"Somethin' to eat, huh? Bring me the fuckin' bag!"

I hesitate, causing her to yell again.

"I said bring me the muthafuckin' bag!"

I walk over to her at a snail's pace, not wanting her to steal my dinner.

She sticks her hand in my bag and pulls out the ham and cheese hoagie, looks at the $2.99 price sticker, then snatches the bag roughly out of my hand. "You lying to me again, huh?" she asks, then stands up.

I take a step back. "No, Mama. I found change in my room, and...uh...I—" I start to stammer.

Smack!

I take another step back, my left cheek stinging something fierce.

She looks through the bag, and an angry look comes over her face. She knows as well as I do that I couldn't have gotten so much with a little loose change. "You think you so slick, don't you, you little whore? You been stealing from me?"

Smack!

"No, Mama! I found that money on my floor!" I continue to lie.

She grabs hold of my hair with her left hand and punches me in the face with her right, before slinging me over the raggedy coffee table. "You fucking steal from me, bitch?" she screams, mercilessly beating me in the back of the head with her fist.

"I didn't steal from you, Mommy! Please stop!" I can taste salty, metallic blood in my mouth, and my nose is busted. A sigh exits my mouth in relief when I see her turn and walk away. That feeling is short-lived, though, and my eyes almost

pop out of my head when she comes back with a thick brown extension cord.

She lifts her arm above her head before bringing it down full force, hitting me on the leg.

"*Aaaaaah!*" I shout.

She strikes me again, this time across my back.

I try desperately to get in a position that won't allow her to do as much damage, but no matter what way I move, it hurts. It feels as if my skin is peeling off.

"*I...bet...you...won't...*" She swings and swings, hitting me all over my body. "*You ain't gonna steal from me! No! Goddamn...more!*"

Swat! Swat!

"*You little ungrateful bitch!*"

"*Mama, I'm sorry!*" I apologize. I know I didn't do anything wrong, but I'll say anything to get her to stop hitting me.

Swat! Swat!

One more hit, and something in me snaps. I can't take no more. I've done nothing wrong, and I'm tired of being treated like shit! My body stings, and I can smell the blood in the air as I somehow push myself up from off the floor. She continues to swing, but I don't even feel the hits anymore. I reach out and push the cruel woman back with all my might, trying to get her to stop.

She falls onto the couch, a bit dazed at first, but the shock on her face wears off quickly, and she jumps back to her feet and starts swinging the cord like a madwoman.

When I feel a sting on my face, I really lose it and start to attack her ass. I grab hold of the cord and yank it, trying to remove it from her hands. Since she's older and has been *smoking dope on my dime and abusing her body for years, she's no match for me. Before she knows it, I've managed to take the cord away from her.*

"What the fuck you going to do with that?" she taunts.

"This!" I pull my hand as far back as I can before bringing it down on her leg. It makes me feel good to hear her finally yell out in pain, to give the bitch a taste of her own nasty, hurtful medicine.

"Stop, Brandy! What the fuck are you doing? I'm yo' mama, for God's sake, and a child ain't s'posed to—"

I ignore her cries and continue to punish her just like she was doing to me—only she deserves it and I didn't.

I hit her about six times before she jumps up and rushes me, causing us both to fall back into the wall. Her fingernails claw at my face, and she jabs her thumbs into my eyes. I reach out and grab her dingy t-shirt and use it to sling her ass to the floor. Once she's down, I run over to her and stomp a mud hole in her no-good ass. As I look down at that woman, I don't see my mother anymore. All I see is the bitch who's been hurting me and using me for all these years, pimping me out for her drug money. Once I get all that hate and revenge out of my system, I pick up my bag and turn to walk away.

"Bitch, I'll kill you!" I hear her say before I feel a sharp pain in the back of my head that instantly gives me a headache.

My hand involuntarily shoots up to the painful spot, and when I pull it away, it's covered with blood. I don't know what she hit me with, but I don't have to wonder long, because I see her swinging around the cement ashtray she uses when she smokes her nasty-smelling cigarettes. Without thinking, before she can hit me with it again, I push her back with everything I've got in me. I can do nothing but watch in horror as my mother falls and hits her head hard against the coffee table with a sickening thud. *Suddenly, the room is eerily quiet, and my mama's not moving at all or saying a word.*

Scared that she's going to get up any second and make good on her promise to kill me, I rush into my room and lock the door behind me. My hands shake as I think about what she's going to do to me when she wakes up. I know she's gonna kill me for sure this time—and all over a damn sandwich and some Oreos.

About an hour goes by before I open the door and peek out. I know something's wrong when I see her still lying in the same position in the same spot, like she hasn't moved an inch. I walk over to her slowly and bend down to see if she's breathing. Her chest is rising very slowly, so I place my ear to her nose. Her breathing is so shallow I can barely hear it.

I wonder what I'm gonna do. If she calls the police when she wakes up and tells them I attacked her, they'll probably believe her—since she's the adult—and take me to jail. So many thoughts rush through my mind, the main one being that I don't want to get in trouble. I'm not sure what's coming over me, but it's like the thoughts pouring into my mind aren't mine. I scramble to pick up anything I may have lost during our fight and drag Mama back over to the couch.

I pick up the empty syringe from the floor, then go in the kitchen and grab a cup out of the cabinet. I fill the cup halfway with bleach and then add ammonia and gently mix the strong-smelling concoction together with a spoon, my eyes and nose burning all the while. I attempt to hold my breath as I stir, but it's no use, and before long, I'm coughing uncontrollably. Once I'm convinced it's mixed enough, I dip the needle in and pull the plunger back as far as I can, filling it up with the noxious, toxic liquid. I walk back over to where my mother is lying on the couch, pick up her arm, and tie it off with a big piece of rubber tubing from the coffee table, just like I've seen her do many times before. Right away, her purple veins begin to pop out at me, and I decided the biggest one that is bulging out the farthest is the one I'll use.

Sure, I'm here physically, but it's as if my body's moving on autopilot, without my soul or mind actually having any control. It's sort of like I'm sitting in the audience watching myself on the big screen, through someone else's eyes.

A small droplet of blood comes out when I stick the needle into the protruding vein, but I don't let it stop me. I push down on plunger, filling my mother's body with the poisonous substance. As soon as the syringe is empty, I pull the needle out, causing blood to spurt, barely missing my face because I forgot to remove the tie-off. I yank that off of her and grab a tissue from the table, then apply pressure to stop the flow. Her blood vessels have been through this drill many, many times before, and they're quick to cooperate, so the bleeding stops quickly and begins to coagulate right next to her other scars and scabs and drug tracks.

I wrap the needle up inside the tissue, then run to the bathroom and flush them both down the toilet before rinsing out the cup I used.

Seconds later, as if on cue, a knock comes at the door, but I ignore it. Instead of answering it, I go into my room to eat, like nothing ever happened.

Hours later, I exit my room to go to the bathroom for a shower to wash away the blood caked in my hair from the ashtray assault. As I walk past my mother, I don't feel a bit of remorse for what I've done. Deep down, I know she deserved it.

Cachet

After my shower, I get dressed and lie down on the floor. I try to drift off to sleep, but I can't. Instead, the day's events hit me like a ton of bricks, and I cry like there's no tomorrow for me, just like there won't be for her. I can't believe I did that to my mother! I can't believe she's lying dead in the next room because of me! A thousand questions start to swirl through my head: What's gonna happen to me? Will they send me to jail? If not, who'll take care of me? It was all because I took my hard-earned money and went to the store to buy some dinner. I don't know why she had to mess with me. All I wanted to do was eat, like normal people do every day, but she wouldn't even let me do that.

* * *

Days go by, and I don't do anything but sit inside my room while my mother stays right there in our front room. I don't know what to do or who to call. I haven't even been out to see if she's dead or alive, but I'm pretty sure she's dead, because I haven't heard a peep from her. People have been knocking on the door, but I refuse to answer.

My body is getting weaker by the day because I haven't eaten or drank anything. I just keep dozing off and waking back up, wondering if I'm going to die here since I don't have anyplace to go or anyone to ask for help. Truth is, without my mama sending men my way, I don't even got a way to earn any money.

Knock! Knock! Knock!

I sit still, figuring it's just a horny trick stopping by for a quickie. As far as I'm concerned, I'm out of business, so they can go get their rocks off somewhere else. There are plenty of other hoes around.

HEARTLESS

"Police!"
And just like that, my heart drops...

* * *

When I jump up, my heart's beating fast, and it's hard to breathe. *These fuckin' nightmares are getting more real by the night! I don't know when I'm dreaming or when I'm not!*

I calm down when I see a ray of sunlight peeking through my bedroom window, signaling a new day. A smile creeps over my face when I look to my right and find Xavier sleeping peacefully beside me. I scoot closer and lay my head on his chiseled chest and listen to his heartbeat, which is still much calmer than mine. It feels good to have somebody to wake up next to sometimes. His warm body feels good against mine, and I don't wanna get up. Truth is, I'm scared of these feelings, as they're something I ain't felt for a long time.

I lie there a bit longer, then give him a small peck on the lips and climb out of bed to head to the bathroom so I can make myself presentable to face the day.

The grease from the bacon pops in the skillet beside me as I use a fork to scramble the cheese eggs in the other pan. Two trays are sitting on top of the island and are already set with utensils, grits, French toast, and home fries. I don't know what put me in the mood for breakfast, but I can't wait to eat. Once the eggs and bacon are done, I pour glasses of orange juice for us, then grab the first tray.

"Wake up, sleepy-head," I say, standing over him with tray in hand.

"Good morning," he responds, squinting through sleepy eyes.

"I made you breakfast."

Cachet

"Aw, thanks, baby."

When he sits up, I place the tray onto his lap and make my way back into the kitchen to retrieve mine.

We eat in silence while watching *House Hunters*, one of my favorite shows. This episode is about a family—a husband, wife, and five children—who wants to move out of inner-city New York to some rural community in Jefferson County, Tennessee. The wife says she loves country living and keeps talking about raising horses when she was younger. This gets me thinking about the day before. I had so much fun horseback riding.

I was scared at first, but Xavier promised he wasn't gonna let anything happen me, and that was all I needed to hear. We rode down a few pathways before stopping in a wooded area. When I climbed off my horse, Xavier was standing there with his hand extended, telling me to close my eyes. I did as I was told and walked with him for a while before he told me to open them. When I did, I was floored! Tears rushed into my eyes, as nobody's ever done anything so special for me before. There is a huge, fancy, red blanket lying in the grass, with a bucket of ice, chilling a bottle of champagne, next to two flutes. On the left side of the blanket was a fresh-baked loaf of bread, along with an assortment of cheese, olives, and dips. A crudités was on the opposite side, with asparagus, broccoli, cauliflower, zucchini, and green beans in it. Prosciutto, sliced sausage, prawns, smoked salmon, and anchovies were also laid out, ready for us to enjoy as much as we were already enjoying each other.

"How do you like it?" he asked.

"I don't like it. I love it!" I exclaimed before leaping into his arms and wrapping my legs around his waist. We shared a succulent kiss on the lips before I sincerely said, "Thank you so much, Xavier. No one has ever done anything like this before."

"Only the best for the best."

Xavier sat me down and assisted in helping me remove the Sergio Grasso Bergamo riding boots he'd picked up for me earlier that day. We enjoyed the food, and I felt brand new as we lay there and looked up at the stars for what seemed like hours. When we finally got back to the stable to return the horses, the people who ran the place invited us back anytime.

"What are you thinking about?" Xavier asks, munching on his crunchy bacon.

"Just about how much fun I had yesterday. Thanks again for that," I say before stuffing a forkful of cheese eggs in my mouth.

"You're welcome, but you don't have to thank me. That's how a lady is supposed to be treated."

I remain silent, not knowing what to say.

I climb out of the bed to pick up my ringing cell phone from the other room. It's Sade, letting me know all her offspring are sick and she has to rush them all to the emergency room. I assure her that it's probably just some stomach bug and tell her to call me when she finds out what's up.

As soon as we hang up, I make a quick call and head back into the bedroom to finish breakfast. We sit and watch TV for a while before he tells me he has to go. He promises to call me later, and just like that, he's out the door.

I doze off for a while, but I'm soon awakened by my phone ringing again. *Damn! Who the hell is it now? Can't a girl be left alone for a while?* "Hello?" I answer groggily, not bothering to check the caller ID.

Cachet

"Brandy, they took my babies! They took my babies!" Sade screams in my ear.

My eyes jerk open, and I sit bolt upright in bed, trying to register what she's saying. She's yelling like a crazy person, barely speaking English, and I can't hardly make out what the hell she's carrying on about. "What? Who took your babies, Sade?"

"Some social workers. Oh my God, Brandy! They sayin' I tried to poison 'em, my own babies, but I wouldn't never do nothing like that! I didn't do nothing, Brandy. Why they gon' take my kids away from they mama?" she rants.

"What hospital are you at?"

"The Cleveland Clinic."

"I'm on my way!"

I hang up the receiver and jump out of bed, then hurry to my truck. I make it to the hospital in record time, even in the ridiculous traffic.

As soon as Sade sees me, she falls into my arms, crying hysterically. She explains that she brought all the kids in because they were throwing up constantly and didn't want to eat anything, which isn't at all like them. The doctors and nurses in the E.R. examined them all individually and determined that they'd eaten something that had made them sick. All six of them had to have their stomach pumped, and upon further investigation, the hospital personnel discovered they'd somehow ingested bleach.

"They asked me all kinds of questions about how they coulda got into some damn Clorox, and I told them I ain't got no idea, 'cause I don't. Why are they doing this to me? I love my kids!" She weeps on my shoulder.

I can't do anything but sit there, so I finally ask, "Is everyone going to be all right?"

"I-I don't know. Brandy, they won't even let me see my babies. They think I did this 'cause…well, because of what happened before."

"You mean when Lavelle swallowed bleach a few years ago?" I ask, recalling the incident she told me about just shortly after we met. She claimed she was cleaning up and the kid mistook the clear liquid for a cup of water and drank it. She convinced the social workers then that it was just an accident, but they warned her it better not happen again, and now it has—this time with all six of them.

"Yeah, and now they think I did it to all of them. I would never do anything to hurt my babies. You gotta believe me, Brandy."

"Of course I do," I assure her.

CHAPTER 9

W hen I return from the hospital, I go into my bathroom and fill my tub with hot water, desperate to
relax after the day I've had. After listening to Sade rant and
rave about her kids, I'm totally drained. I sit on my bed and
use my middle and index fingers to rub my temples in a slow,
circular motion, trying to relieve the throbbing pain that's
lurking in my head. The two Advil I popped a little while ago
haven't done shit to help at all.

I kick my shoes off and lie back on my bed, close my eyes,
and think about the events that transpired today. I can't believe
they hauled Sade off to jail for assault, but her ass really flipped
the fuck out! We had been sitting in the waiting room for a
little over an hour before we received an update.

The extremely young-looking black social worker, who
gives off a vibe like she thinks she's better than everybody else,
strutted into the waiting room dressed to the nines. I instantly
felt underdressed in my Juicy Couture jogging outfit I had on
and wished I'd done my normal morning routine, 'cause she
was shittin' on me, looking like that. Her hair is jet black, cut in
a short cropped style, with a feathered bang. The black Donna

Karan pencil skirt with the matching knit cardigan fit her just right: form fitting, but not too tight. A short pair of pearls sat on top of a cream cashmere turtleneck, and her feet were dressed in some Manolo Blahnik leopard-print pumps that echoed loudly on the tile floor as she walked. I know her whole outfit must've cost a couple grand on the low side. I don't know what ol' girl does on the side, but I for damn sure know that her social work job don't pay her enough to dress that way. In any case, li'l mama was fly as fuck, and I felt like yesterday's garbage in what I was wearing.

Anyway, she introduced herself as Ms. Perry, and she was escorted by two police officers who looked pissed off to be there. In a very nasty tone, she told Sade that she won't be getting her children back anytime soon. She basically accused her of being an abusive, neglectful, horrible parent who has no business having or raising kids. At first I didn't understand why the police were there, but I quickly realized it was because this Ms. Perry has a smart-ass mouth and a nasty attitude. It pissed me off how she talked to Sade; not only was it unprofessional, but it was also uncalled for. The police informed Sade that she'll be more than likely brought up on neglect charges, since it's the second time something like this has happened to her children in her care.

"I love my kids!" Sade cried out as tears ran down her face and fell into her lap.

"If you love your children so much, why are they here, fighting for their lives?" Ms. Perry asked smartly.

"I've got no clue, but it's not my fault. I've done nothing wrong," Sade said, trying to plead her case. "Since the last time it happened, I don't even keep bleach or anything else that might hurt or poison them anywhere in their reach. If I even have any of that stuff in the house, it's up on very high shelves that I can barely reach myself."

"So you say," Ms. Perry snapped, rolling her eyes.

"You don't have to be so evil," I said, mean-mugging her; the smart-mouth bitch was working my nerves.

"Well, excuse me if I'm not smiling and happy. There are six sick little kids back there, and your friend here is to blame." She pointed her manicured figure at Sade. "My job is to protect them from monsters like her here, who shouldn't even be able to breed. Neglectful mothers and fathers like this make me sick, and I'm going to do *everything* in my power to make sure she—"

"I'm tired of you, bitch!" Sade screamed, cutting her off.

Ms. Perry didn't see it coming, and before she knew what was happening, there was a loud cracking sound. I looked on in shock as I watched Sade hit the woman in the face repeatedly with one of those heavy-ass hospital phones. The police officers snatched Sade off the woman by the back of her shirt and attempted to put her in handcuffs, but that was no easy task, because she was like a caged animal, punching and kicking, trying to get back at her victim. By the time they got the cuffs on her, Ms. Perry was unconscious, her face covered in blood; it was a good thing we were still close to the E.R., because she was in such bad shape that the orderlies had to lift her up on the gurney and cart her off for treatment. Another set of officers showed up and asked me a few questions before allowing me to go on my way, and I let them know I ain't have nothing to do with that shit!

After undressing and wrapping my hair, I dip my foot inside the tub to test the temperature. When I'm convinced it's not too hot, I step in and submerge my body, all the way up to my shoulders. I hit the button to turn on the jets, and they come to life, massaging my body with just the right amount of pressure. It feels so good and is exactly what I need at this moment. I lean back and rest my head on my terrycloth bath pillow and close my eyes. Unfortunately, I drift back into Dream Land, which is not a place I wanna be.

* * *

2001...

Bam! Bam! Bam! Bam!

The police continue to bang on the door.

I cover my ears with both hands in an attempt to drown out the noise, but it's no use. It just keeps getting louder and louder, and they aren't giving up. Suddenly, I find myself very, very scared—maybe more scared than I've ever been in my young life, and I've had some close calls before. I hear the door being kicked it, but I don't move. I just sit there like a frightened little puppy, quivering and not moving from my spot.

"We've got a female on the couch, deceased," I hear a man say before the doorknob twists. "Anybody in here?" he asks.

Tears stream down my face. I know they're coming to get me, and I'm sure I'm going to jail for what I've done.

"Hey, there's a kid back here!" another officer yells after kicking my thin bedroom door in. "You okay, sweetheart?"

I say nothing and continue to sit there.

Everything from then on is a blur to me. My mother is dead, and they end up taking me to the hospital, where I'm diagnosed with and treated for a concussion, malnutrition, and dehydration—all courtesy of my neglectful, abusive, drug-addicted mama.

HEARTLESS

* * *

I've been in the hospital for a little over a week. A few detectives came in once to ask me a few questions, but I didn't tell them a thing. Nobody blames me for what happened to Mama. I guess they figure she got into a fight with someone, and they gave her bad dope, and if that's what they wanna think, I'll let 'em. Far as I'm concerned, I'm free from that life now, and I don't hafta worry about having sex with anybody else for money ever again.

A middle-aged white nurse walks into the room, but I don't bother to acknowledge her. She calls my name, but I don't even give eye contact and just continue to stare off into space. When she realizes she's wasting her time, she blurts out that she has a surprise for me. My face shows no excitement. After all, I don't even know this woman, and in my experience, surprises are never a good thing.

Just then, a very tall guy walks in behind her. He's dark as night, wearing blue jeans and a white t-shirt, and I don't recognize him from Adam.

"This is your father, Brandy," The nurse introduces.

I know this must be some sort of joke, so I ask, "Who?" Now that I think about it, that's the first word I've spoken since I was admitted and they put that cold backless gown on me that leaves my ass hanging out.

"My name is Pitch. I'm your daddy," the tall man says before she has a chance to repeat herself. He smiles, showing off the one gold tooth in his mouth. "I'm here to take you home—with me. You're my daughter, baby, and I'm going to show you how a princess is s'posed to be treated."

I'm sure he doesn't even realize it, but his words are music to my ears. Nobody's ever called me a princess before, and I sure hope he's not lyin'.

* * *

Two days later, we pull up at the all-brick Tudor in Akron, and my jaw just drops. I'm shocked to discover my father's been living so lavishly when I couldn't even afford to eat. The place is huge, with a circular driveway so big he could probably park twenty cars in it.

When we walk inside, I'm so excited I can hardly contain myself. Finally, I've got a nice place to call home, and I can't believe my good luck.

A beautiful lady walks down the large staircase and right up to us, then introduces herself as Trixie, my daddy's girlfriend. I can't tell what ethnicity she is, but she sure ain't black. She puts me in the mind of Pocahontas, with long, jet-black hair that stops just above her butt. Her skin is the color of butterscotch, and she has an oval face, slanted eyes, and a small nose like mine. There's some kind of exotic look about her, and I can see why my father chose her to be his girl, because she's absolutely beautiful.

Trixie gives me a tour of the house. The place has six bedrooms, five full bathrooms, and two half-baths. She is so nice to me and even shows me to my room, like I'm some kind of special guest.

When I walk inside my new bedroom, I can't believe my eyes. It's decorated in mostly black, and everything looks expensive. The comforter even matches the curtains, and I've never had a comforter or curtains before! My father put the place together nicely, and I'm thrilled to be here.

I am even more excited when I open the huge closet, which

is about as big as my old room! It's completely jam-packed with clothes, and I won't have to worry about too-little, ratty old tennis shoes or dollar store flip-flops that are two sizes too small, 'cause my father stockpiled my closet with shoes for days!

Even with all the expensive things in the room, the best part about the whole thing is that it's actually mine—all mine! From here on out, I'll be sleeping in a real bed, not lying on the floor under a nasty old sleeping bag, hoping rats won't bite my toes. I feel so special, knowing he went to all this trouble for me, and I'm beginning to feel like the princess he tells me I am.

* * *

Pitch is absolutely amazing. As time goes on, he buys me everything I want and spoils me rotten. I'm a daddy's little girl now, something I've always dreamt of.

Trixie has become a second mother to me—much more of a mama than my own ever was—and I look up to her. She's taught me how to be a woman and how to carry myself. Shaving my legs and under my arms are a must and should be done at least twice a week, she says. She showed me how to put on makeup and walk in heels and all the other things my real mother never bothered to teach me. I don't even have to worry about my nappy old ponytails, because Trixie buys me relaxers and takes me to get my hair done.

Matter fact, I spend most of my time with Trixie, but that don't really bother me, because she's cool. She says Dad isn't around much because he has to handle his business. He does stop in here and there to give me money, and he told his driver he has to take me shopping at least once a week.

Cachet

* * *

By the time I'm thirteen, my body has bloomed, and I'm starting to take on the build of a grown woman. My thighs are a nice size, I've got quite a booty, and my breasts are full and round. My closet's full of grown-up clothes, like tight jeans, short skirts, and revealing tops. I only own one pair of tennis shoes, a pair of white Air Maxx, because all I wear most of the time are heels and boots. My dressers are full of sexy panty-and-bra sets, and my vanity drawers are full of perfume and makeup.

I never question why they let me dress so provocatively, because I like being treated like a grown-up. I just figure Pitch likes giving me my freedom, so I'm happy to take it! I don't even have to go to school, because I do all my work on the Internet, so I'm never really around any girls my age. I'm in heaven and couldn't be happier, but just like the saying goes, all good things must come to an end.

* * *

Two months before my fourteenth birthday, the shit hits the fan.

A few days after Christmas, Pitch calls me into the bedroom that he shares with Trixie. When I walk in, I find him sitting at his desk with his back to me. He's dressed in a black silk robe, and he has a piece of paper in his hand.

"You wanted to see me?" I ask, getting his attention and causing him to turn around and face me. "What's wrong, Daddy?" I ask, noticing the sad look on his face.

"I've got bad news, baby. We're gonna lose the house, the cars, and everything else I've worked so hard for," he tells me sadly.

"What? Why?" I screech, sure that I heard him wrong.

"I'm in debt, Brandy. It's…bad."

"I don't understand. What happened?"

"I've spent way too much money buying you all those expensive things. I wanted to give you what you didn't have growing up and show you the life you shoulda been living. I've spent everything I have in the process. Now, if I don't come up with something soon, we're gonna be put out, and you'll probably be sent to a foster home."

"That can't happen, Daddy! I don't wanna leave you. I love you!" I cry out, running over to him. I place my arms around his neck and hug him tight. "I'll give everything back, even all my Christmas gifts, as long as I don't have to leave this place!"

"I can't do that. That shit I got you for Christmas was just a drop in the bucket compared to all the other money I've spent. God, what am I gonna do?" I unclasp my arms and take a step back.

When he puts his head down on the desk, I feel so bad. It feels like this is all my fault. I remember every time I went shopping. Never once did I stop to think about all the money I was spending, and I feel selfish now.

I turn my head in the direction of Trixie when she walks into the room. She sashays over to the bed and takes a seat, then reaches up to remove the scrunchie from her hair.

It resembles silk as it falls gracefully, landing in the arch of her back. I stare at her with tears running down my face, trying to figure out how we're going get out of this mess.

"What's going on?" she asks.

Neither Pitch nor I say a word, and I direct my eyes down

to my French tips that I just got filled yesterday.

Silence ensues for at least two more minutes before he looks up like he has an idea, and my ears peak with anticipation. "I'm gonna have to put you to work, Brandy."

More silence.

"You're not a kid anymore, and it's time you start carrying your weight around here."

"Carrying my weight?" I ask, confused.

"Yes, carrying your weight."

"Where do you want me to work? Are you talking about McDonald's or something, Daddy? I can go down there and fill out an application tomorrow if you want." Even though I'm not looking forward to flipping burgers and salting fries, I'm excited that I'll somehow be able to help fix this mess I've made, being so greedy.

"McDonald's? No, baby. They don't pay enough. I've got something else in mind."

"Okay. What, Daddy?"

Once again, there's silence.

"Daddy, what is it? What do you have in mind?" I ask again.

"The track, Brandy."

"What!? You want me to sell my body!?" I yell, sure I heard him wrong. I know exactly what the track is, because my mother always threatened to send me out there whenever she thought I was acting too grown.

"Yes, but only for a little while, sweetheart—just till I get these bills caught up. Like I said, I spent all my money spoiling you, trying to give you what you never had. I shouldn't have, but you're my princess," he says, laying the guilt trip on thick.

"But I-I'm you daughter," I say, my feelings clearly hurt.

"You've always said I'm a princess, Daddy."

I glance over at Trixie, who's still sitting on the bed. She drops her head and starts to cry bitterly, sobbing and sniffling as tears pour out of her dark eyes, but she doesn't say a word.

"I know, baby, and trust me when I tell you it's killing me to even have to suggest it, but I don't see any other way."

"It must not be killin' you too much, Daddy, because you're sure as hell asking, ain't you?" I snap.

"Brandy, that's not fair. All I've ever tried to do since I brought you here was make you happy, and you're gonna repay me with that kind of lip? You're going to get mad at me when I need your help after everything I've done for you, pulling you out of that hellish life you were living with your bitch of a mama?"

I know he's right, as much as I hate to admit it. I was never happy until I came here, and he's never asked anything of me before. Hell, I ain't even had to wash a dish or do my own laundry. "You sure there's no other way?" I ask, defeated.

He shakes his head. "Uh-uh, baby. I've racked my brain, but I know nothing else is gonna get us as much money as we need as quick as we need it. I need your help, Brandy."

My eyes well with tears, and I look at him in disbelief. "Daddy, there's gotta be something else. I can't—"

"Damn it, Brandy, didn't I just say there's no other way? Now please stop asking me so many damn questions!" he yells.

I jump, because he's never raised his voice to me before. As I sit there, pondering his change of character, it hits me like a ton of bricks. My daddy dearest has been planning this all along. I know it's not about him needing money. If it was, he'd ask Trixie to hit the track, because she's gorgeous and probably a lot more experienced than me. Besides that, she's actually grown. I can't imagine why in the world a man would ask his thirteen-year-old daughter, his own flesh and blood, to sell herself before asking his girlfriend, who's no blood relation. He must think I'm a fool or something, but I'm definitely not that. "No. I'm not doing it," I say firmly, meaning every word.

"You really don't have a choice."

The look on his face tells me he's not bluffing, but I don't care. I refuse to sell my body again. If he wants to kick me out, he can, but I'm not anybody's whore—and especially not my father's. "I do have a choice, and I said I'm not fuckin' doing it!" I scream. I don't care that I just cursed my dad out, because I'm old enough to stand my ground.

"Trixie, give us a minute."

"Not now, Pitch," my makeshift mama says, wearing a worried look on her face. "She's too young, just a baby really, and it ain't right for you to—"

"I wasn't askin' you," Pitch says, glaring at her. "Get the fuck outta here right now, or I'll throw you out."

Still, Trixie doesn't move.

"Bitch, if you make me get up out this chair, yo' ass is gonna get it worse than her. I said to get the fuck outta here!" he roars in a voice I've never heard coming from his mouth before.

Knowing he means business, Trixie climbs off the bed and walks toward the door. She gives me a look of sympathy before she walks out and closes the door behind her.

"Now, what the fuck did you just say to me?" Pitch asks as he gets up from his office chair and walks toward me.

I swallow the lump in my throat and answer, "I'm not doin—"

But before I can get the words out of my mouth all the way, he wraps his hands tightly around my neck. "Listen here, you little ungrateful bitch. You're gonna do whatever the fuck I tell you to do." His breath is hot on the side of my face, and he has this wild look in his eyes—a look I've never seen from him before.

It's hard for me to breathe, so I attempt to loosen his grip by prying his fingers off my neck, breaking two of my acrylic nails in the process. Just when I think I'm about to pass out, my father releases me and lets me fall on the floor. My hands move to the spot where his just were as I struggle to catch my breath. He takes a step toward me, and I scoot back until I'm in the corner of the room. I feel like prey, trapped by a predator, and the only thing I can think to do is attack. As soon as he moves close enough, I lift my right foot up and kick him in the nuts as hard as I can.

Once he's lying on the floor, writhing and moaning in pain and holding his junk where my foot made contact, I make a run for the door. Just as I try to step over him, he reaches out and grabs hold of my ankle, causing me to fall and hit my head on the dresser. Next thing I know, my head is spinning and my vision is blurry, but the thought of him choking me again gives me the strength to continue to fight. I kick my feet at him violently, trying to make him release his tight hold on my leg. I connect and land one that busts his lip open.

"You fuckin' bitch!" he yells before standing up and kicking me in the ribs.

I roll over on my side and cry out from the pain of the blow. "Trixie!" I shout. "Trixie, please help me!"

"Nobody can help you now," he growls. "Least of all that mouthy bitch."

Cachet

He climbs on top of me and puts all his weight on my chest, then smacks me in the face with the back of his hand; my mouth fills with blood. The heaviness of his body on my upper torso makes it hard for me to breathe, so I stop fighting, hoping he'll finally roll off and leave me alone.

"Yo' ass is gonna learn obey what I say. Whether it's the easy way or the hard way, you are gonna learn!"

He stands up, and I double over in pain when he kicks me in the stomach. It feels as if I have to throw up, only nothing comes out. He walks over to his desk calmly and grabs a Kleenex to dab the blood from his lip. Meanwhile, I lie in the same spot, wondering if he's gonna come back to hit me or kick me again.

When he walks into the bathroom, I make a run for the door again, knowing I have to get out of his house. I'm almost down the hall when my head is jerked back by the hair, and the next thing I know, my whole body is slammed on the floor like some kind of pro wrestler is having his way with me. My shoulders and back are suddenly on fire; the hall carpet causes severe rug burn on my skin as my jerk-ass father drags me back toward his bedroom. I kick and scream and scratch the whole way, but it does no good and only seems to make him angrier.

Once we're inside, he closes and locks the door, then places the small key in the pocket of his robe. "You a hardheaded li'l bitch, ain't you? You musta got that shit from your strung-out mother, but I ain't gon' put up with it. I'm about to show you what happens to li'l bitches who think they bad and won't listen to me."

He reaches down and snatches my cotton shorts, and I can only pray he's not about to do what I'm thinking. Next, he tugs on my t-shirt, and I struggle to push his big, strong, rough hands away. A solid punch to the face catches me right in the eye, and I see enough stars to take the fight out of me. Completely overpowered and hurting inside and out, I can't do nothing but lie back and let the man do whatever it is he plans to do. Another punch connects with my nose, and my hand instinctively moves up in a feeble attempt to block the next one, but it does no good. He rains punches down on me left and right, even though I'm too weak to fight anymore.

Finally, he gets up and walks away, only to return with a leather strap. I don't even fight back when he reaches down and pulls my shirt off, leaving me on the floor in my panties and bra.

"Please don't!" I cry, but my pleas fall on deaf ears.

Whack!

Pitch brings the strap down full force, the same way my mama did with that extension cord so many months ago. The first hit stings, but I don't have time to dwell on it too long before another one follows.

Whack!

"You think you bad? Is that it?" he taunts as he continues to swing the strap, hitting me all over my body.

"I-I'm sorry, Daddy! I'm sorry!"

"Not as sorry as yo'li'l ass gonna be!"

Whack!

I scramble on all fours, trying to get away, but that only results in lashes landing all over my back.

"Don't run now!" he yells like a madman. After the longest five minutes of my life, he finally stops and drops the strap on the floor.

I don't flinch when he tears off my panties and bra, even though the pain is more intense than anything I've ever felt. I know there's nothing I can do to stop him, and before I know it, I'm completely naked, welts all over my body. The man who fathered me stands over me and slowly begins to untie the belt of his robe, then lets his garment fall to the floor. When I see that he's not wearing anything under it, I close my eyes; I already know what's coming.

"Don't get scared now, Miss Billy Badass. I got something for ya." He drops to his knees. "I know you're not a virgin, but Daddy's gonna give it to you real good." With no remorse, he plunges roughly into me, causing me to scream out in pain.

I'm dry as a bone, but it doesn't bother him a bit as he rams himself into me repeatedly. The burning feeling is so extreme that it feels as if someone is holding a match between my legs. With the rocking motion of each of his violent, incestuous thrusts, the carpet rubs against the torn flesh on my back, only adding to my pain.

Tears roll slowly out of my eyes as I'm faced with the harsh reality of my life. I know now that there is no escaping it. This is my cruel destiny, and no matter where I turn, I never catch a break. Again I'm shown that there's no point in trusting anybody—even my own blood—because everybody wants something, and that's something I'm not willing to freely give.

* * *

I sit up and look around frantically and only calm down when I realize I'm not thirteen anymore and am safely inside my own home, with that bastard of a daddy nowhere near me. My hands resemble prunes because I've been in the tub so long, and the water has gone cold. I can't believe I fell asleep like that, but it was a rough day, and Xavier's been keeping me pretty busy at night, so I must've been more tired than I thought.

I pull the plug on the tub to release the water, still not believing I fell asleep in there. I stand up and reach for my thick towel and wrap it around my wet, wrinkly body before stepping out and heading into my bedroom.

My heart is still beating rapidly when I sit down on my bed and apply lotion to my body. It's 3 o'clock in the morning, and nothing is on except *Family Matters*, so I laugh at Steve Urkel's silly ass until the TV is watching me sleep.

CHAPTER 10

At around 11 a.m., I drive down Osha's street. While I'm driving, I get a call from an unknown number, and I decide not to answer it, afraid it might be Roger's lonely ass again. The phone finally stops ringing, but then whoever it is calls back, irritating the living hell out of me. *Who the hell is this, and what the fuck do they want, being all relentless and shit?* I pull into the driveway, shut off my engine, and answer with attitude, "Hello!?"

"Hold on," says a rude female with a male-like voice.

Who the fuck is this manly-soundin' bitch?

"Oh my God, Brandy, I'm so happy you answered!" Sade screams.

"Yeah, I been busy. What's up?" I ask.

Sade's been in jail for about a month, and she calls me constantly; my phone's been ringing at least twenty times a day with unknown numbers, and I don't even answer my landline no more because I figure it's just her bothersome ass. Sure, I feel bad for what happened to her with that bitch-ass social worker, but that don't mean I wanna be besties with the low-class Walmart-shopping bitch. I guess she finally got a little smart and had somebody else call just so she can talk to me, but I ain't too fond of the stalking-ass bitch who won't leave me alone. "Tyreak died a few days ago." She pauses. "I need to get outta here ASAP so I can plan my baby's funeral," she says, sniffling and holding back tears.

Much as she pisses me off and disgusts me most of the time, the news tugs at my heart and shocks me. *I never thought it would come to this.*

"Please tell me you have my money. If I've ever needed it, now's the time."

"Sorry, but I ain't got nothing for you," I say dryly. Sure, it's fucked up that her son died and all, but I don't owe her shit, and I sure as hell ain't givin' her another damn dime.

"Huh? What you mean, you ain't got nothing for me?" she asks shocked.

"Just what I said."

"Don't play with me, Brandy. I'm sure the IRS has sent that money by now, and you know I need it. You've got a new excuse every time I ask you, so I'm gonna ask you one more time. Where's the money you owe me from our taxes, when you claimed my kids?"

"You ain't gonna get an excuse from me no' more, but you ain't getting shit from me either," I state matter-of-factly.

"What?"

"Does jail make you hard of hearing or something? Damn. You heard me. I said—"

"Yeah, I heard you, bitch, but you got me fucked up if you think you're gonna get away with not giving me my money!" she screams, mad as hell, the tears long gone.

"Oh? You think you tough, huh, Sade? Girl, I ain't worried in the least about yo' broke ass. Bye!" I yell into the phone before disconnecting the call.

In a huff and sick of her shit, I grab the handle of my leather Prada bag, snatch my keys out of the ignition, and exit my truck.

Ring!

"Damn! What the hell do you want?" I snap into the receiver.

"Bitch you know what I want, and you betta stop playing with me. I want my money!" the incarcerated li'l big-girl-panty-wearing bitch yells in my ear.

I chuckle. I can tell she's pissed, but I also know there ain't nothing she can do about it. "Look, Sade, I'm not giving you no money—not now nor ever again. I ain't heartless, and I'm sorry about what happened to yo' son and everything, but you gonna have to chalk that up as a loss."

"What!? I ain't chalking a muthafuckin' thang, bitch! That's my baby you talking about. You are heartless—heartless as fuck—and trust me when I tell you that you are gonna give me my money, one way or another."

"Listen here, Sade. I'm far from worried about you doing *anything* to me, so you oughtta quit wasting my time and your breath. Keep talkin' all that tough shit if you want, but I still ain't giving you one dollar. That's my money, bitch, and it's yo' loss," I say calmly as I reach out to ring the doorbell.

"I got you, Brandy, but trust me on this. When I get out, which I will, I'm gonna make it my business to stop by and see your ass. You shady as fuck for real, and you know it. My son is dead, and instead of being able to plan his funeral, I'm on the phone arguing with you about my money! It's cool though. See, God don't like ugly, and I know you gonna get what's coming to you—if not from me, from Him. You just betta run like hell, because I'm coming fo' yo' neck!"

"Get out? Girl, you ain't goin' nowhere. Don't you remember what they charged you with? You got a rap sheet so long that it don't make no sense—child endangerment, aggravated assault and battery, resisting arrest, and now murder. Your hot-temper ass assaulted a government worker, and you've been accused of poisoning your kids, one of whom is now dead. Are you too dumb to realize the hot water you're in? Without a good lawyer, which I know you can't afford, your chances of getting out in this lifetime are slim to none. They don't let violent-ass, psycho child murderers back out on the street. Sade, I hate to tell you, but you know you fucked with the public defender they're gonna assign to you. Sorry, boo, but you're shit out of luck. Like I said before, I ain't scared. Got no reason to be."

"You fucking bitch!"

Osha opens the door and greets me with a hug.

"You ready?" I ask, ignoring the hell out of Sade, who's still yelling pointless threats in my damn ear.

"Yeah. C'mon in. I just need a few minutes," Taz's woman says.

After she jogs up the stairs, I head toward the back of the house. In the family room, I see Taz, sitting on the couch with Zema's man Dan, playing some sort of shooter game on the Xbox 360. I don't say a word to either of them, and I don't pay Dan any mind as he gives me all types of winks and sexy faces. I ain't even thinking about his ass, but he just doesn't seem to take the hint.

As I take a seat on the cream-colored sectional, close to the window and away from the gamers, Sade just keeps on yelling in my ear. "I'm gonna call the IRS, and they're gonna get you, bitch! You just wait and see."

"Girl, you crazy. The IRS ain't got no more time than I do to listen to some sorry excuse for a mother who neglects her children, the same pitiful mama who's responsible for the death of her son."

"I've never neglected my kids, and you know that, Brandy. I would never do anything to hurt them, and I think it's pretty fucked up that you're talking about my baby like that when he just passed away a few days ago. I love them with everything in me, and I'm not a sorry excuse for a mother." She sniffles.

"Yeah, yeah," I say, brushing her off. "Look, I gotta go, but before I do, let me leave you with this. If you love your damn brats so much, don't ask someone you barely know to babysit them, and especially not to feed them. They might just gobble up something that could get you in a whole lotta trouble." I laugh.

"What? What did you just say?" she asks. When I don't say anything, she continues with the interrogation. "What are you talking about? Brandy, did you put bleach in my kids' food? Oh my God! Brandy, what the hell did you do?" she asks, confused. "Tell me you didn't do no shit like that. Please tell me you didn't hurt my babies. Naw, no way. Surely you ain't do no shit like that to my children, Brandy. You said you love kids and that they remind you of your sister's and—"

"I do, and I don't know what you're talking about, Sade."

"Tell me you didn't do it, Brandy. Please say you didn't. I'm begging you. Shit, I can't take this, Brandy!"

Silence ensues, because I ain't telling her shit. One confession is enough for one day.

"I trusted you! I invited you into my house, into our lives, and let you be around my babies. How could you do something like this to them? My son is dead because of you! You hear me, bitch? My fuckin' little boy done took his last breath because of yo' triflin', psycho ass, and my other babies have been in pain and taken off to some foster care. Do you even give a fuck?" she screams.

"Sade, you clearly trippin, so I'm about to hang up. I wish you luck. Just be careful in jail. I heard it's some crazy lesbo bitches in there, so don't drop the soap." I giggle.

Just then, Osha walks into the family room with her purse on her arm, letting me know that she's ready.

"I'ma kill you, bitch! I'm gonna fucking kill you. You just wait and see! Nobody fucks with my kids, Brandy. Yo' sick ass is dead. Do you hear me, bitch? My people are gonna see you, ho, and when they do, they gon' fuck yo' shit all the way up. I swear on my baby's life, I'm gonna fucking kill—"

Click.

I hang up my phone and put an end to her babbling, because she's starting to give me a headache, and I'm fresh out of Advil.

"Damn! Who was that?" Osha asks, laughing. "She sure was flipping out on yo' ass. She made my ears hurt!"

"Girl, that was Sade's dumb ass, and she ain't gonna do shit but run her mouth," I say, rolling my eyes in frustration.

I take this moment to catch a look at what Osha's wearing. I gotta laugh to myself, because ol' Miss Plain Jane never dresses up, no matter where we go. She always looks like a teenager, not a grown-ass woman. This time ain't no exception with her cuffed denim shorts, a white wife-beater, and a pair of white Dior thong sandals. Her hair is parted down the middle and pulled into two braided ponytails, held in place by little white flower clips that probably belong to her twin little girls.

Don't get me wrong: She looks cute, and it ain't like I'm embarrassed to be seen with her or some shit like I would be with Sade's trashy ass, just not *adult* cute.

I, on the other hand, am doing it like a grown woman in my cute-ass burgundy BOSS black plaid summer dress, with a cream belt and a pair of five-inch peep-toe Giuseppe Zanotti pumps.

"Sade?" Osha says with a look on her face that shows she's in deep thought. A second later, she snaps her fingers, as if she's figured it out. "The girl whose in jail?"

"Yep. That's her."

"What she mad at you for?"

"She's been askin' me for money to bail her ass out. Shit, it ain't my fault she's in there," I say, purposely not giving her the full story. She'll find out soon enough just how grimy I am.

"I feel ya. It's not your responsibility to bond her out. She shoulda thought of that before she assaulted that poor woman. Women these days kill me, always trying to play the victim. I say they oughtta close their damn legs or at least buy a box of condoms and quit having all these damn kids, if they ain't gonna take care of them. It's as simple as that."

"You're right. It don't make no damn sense. Anyway, I'm not going to let her mess up my day with this nonsense. Are you ready to go?"

"Ready when you are."

We walk toward the door, and she bends down in front of Taz and kisses him softly on the lips. He looks around her head at me, probably trying to see if I'm gonna get upset, but all I do is wink. As soon as Osha politely bids Dan farewell, we're out the door and on our way to the Beachwood Mall to find something for our Vegas vacation.

Cachet

We're planning to leave for Sin City at the beginning of next week, and I couldn't be more excited about getting my ass out of Ohio and doing a little gambling. I'm hoping to win a little money and figure out a lick or two to fatten up my bank account. What happens in Vegas might stay in Vegas most of the time, but I'm sure as hell planning to bring some of that drama home, because my real mission is to execute my plan to get Osha out of the way. After that, Taz will be all mine, till I get everything I want to take from his ass. When I'm through with him, he can go on and go about his business. Hell, I don't even care if he ends up crawling back home to Osha once I've dried his ass out.

"If your girl only knew that you was trying to get with me, what would she do? If your girl only knew that you were dissin' her to talk to me…"

I looked over at Osha, before answering my ringing phone, then place it in my left ear. "What's up, baby?"

"Why you ain't speak to me before you left?" Taz asks.

"I didn't want to bother you." I giggle as I glance at Osha out the corner of my eye. She's looking at me, trying to eavesdrop, but I discreetly turn the volume down so she can't hear her man's voice.

"Stop playing with me, girl. Next time yo' ass sees me, you betta have something to say," he demands with attitude; I don't mind a bit, and I sorta like it when he gets upset.

"You need to do the same then, honey."

"Brandy, don't make me fuck you up. You're straight up pissing me off," he says, then pauses slightly. When he speaks again, his voice is softer. "I miss yo' pretty ass."

I smile. "Yeah, I hear you."

"I'm for real, baby. When can I see you?" he asks.

I purposely refuse to answer him right away, enjoying the game.

"Brandy!"

"Huh?"

"What the hell you doing, girl? I just asked you a question."

"Oh. I'm sorry, baby. This fine-ass nigga in the car beside me just got me all mesmerized, that's all."

Osha has to laugh out loud, because she knows I ain't seen no damn body besides us and a morbidly obese Pepsi truck driver.

"You think that shit's funny? I'm happy you think everything is a joke. Bye!" Taz yells before hanging up in my ear.

I reach for my charger and plug my phone in, then set in the cup holder.

"Who was that?" Osha asks with a sly smile on her face.

"This dude I mess with from time to time," I say nonchalantly.

"Really? I haven't heard you say anything about him."

"That's because he's already got a woman he lives with."

"Brandy! You know that shit's just...salty and wrong." she says in a serious voice like some school teacher, trying to scold me.

"Yeah, I know, but she must not be doing something right, because he's steady trying to fuck with me. He's all up in my face every chance he gets, and I'm sure his girl don't know. Hence the ringtone."

She laughs like a fool, not even realizing she's the dumbass girl I'm talking about.

"Shit, that nigga spends the night with me more often than she knows. She's a damn fool."

"Hmm. I guess you're right. Maybe she's got a man or

Cachet

something on the side or she just don't care. It's gotta be one or the other, 'cause if my man were up to some shit, you bet your ass I'd know."

I almost laugh out loud but manage to stifle that shit, knowing it will give me away. "Naw, this bitch is just dumb, but that's neither here nor there. Now c'mon. Let's buy this bitch out!" I say as I maneuver my truck into a parking space at the mall.

* * *

I'm glad we started shopping early, because we spent a good five hours buying everything for our trip. I'm exhausted by the time we're done, and I swear Saks Fifth Avenue made a come-up today. I spent almost $30,000, and I'm not sure exactly how much Osha spent, but she couldn't have been too far behind me. She didn't seem to give a fuck how much anything cost, 'cause she was spending Taz's money left and right. What she don't know is that I was also shopping on his dime, so I really didn't give a fuck how much I spent either.

I damn near picked out everything for Osha. If it were up to that girl, she'd have bought nothing but shorts, tanks, and flip-flops, and nobody wears shit like that in Vegas. I had to force her dull ass to sexy it up a bit. We're going on a girls' trip, and I want to have some real-ass fun. She allowed me to dress her, but not without complaining every once in a while. I really don't give a shit though, 'cause she ain't going nowhere with me, looking like my little sister. I didn't tell her so, but she has to dress grown or stay her ass at home—period.

After we lug all the bags to the truck, we head back inside the mall to grab something to eat from Maggiano's Little Italy. Once we're seated, our waitress—a young Puerto Rican girl dressed in black slacks, a white, long-sleeved shirt, and a black vest—walks up to our table and introduces herself as Eva. Her hair is pulled back in a ponytail, and her bangs are cut short, stopping just above her thick eyelashes. She smiles, revealing a set of deep dimples that only add to her beauty. "What can I get you ladies to drink this afternoon?" she asks in a slight accent.

We give her our orders, and she smiles and quickly walks away.

Twenty minutes later, Eva returns with my Crab and Shrimp Tropheo, garlic potatoes, and sautéed spinach. I'm so damn hungry that I've already got my fork in my hand before she has a chance to walk away; I guess I worked up an appetite spending Taz's money.

We eat and talk excitedly about our upcoming trip. We have reservations at the MGM Grand, in a Skyloft two-bedroom suite, and I just know we're going to have a blast. We'd better, considering how much money Taz has spent on this trip; for me and Osha together, it cost him another thirty grand, though Osha doesn't know he's covering my tab as well as hers.

Osha shares a secret with me: She's excited about leaving, in part, because she needs a break from Taz. She goes on to say she has a feeling in her gut that he's been cheating on her. "I don't know what I'll do if I find out it's true," she says. She does say she'll miss her kids while we're away, but not that much, and that only tells me that being a mother ain't all it's cracked up to be.

For her entire spiel, I barely pay attention, because my mind keeps drifting back to the last time Taz and I had some private time. We were at his house, and he had me spread-eagled on the sofa while he touched the back of my pussy with his tongue. After I squirted my juices all over his face, he laid me across the back of the couch and pounded my ass like a man on a mission, and I loved every minute of it.

Osha nudges me softly on the arm, snapping me out of my daydream. "What you thinking about, girl? I'm over here running my mouth, and yo' ass is off in a daze." She laughs.

"I'm sorry, girl. I was just thinking about my baby. I gotta make sure I hook up with him before we leave next week," I say, moving my lower body as if I'm riding someone in the chair.

"Girl, you're so damn nasty, but I ain't mad at ya. I wish I could get some, but Taz has been so preoccupied that he ain't touched me in almost two weeks. I just know he's been fucking with somebody else, 'cause we used to have sex at least twice a day, and now he acts like I got the damn plague."

I guess he wasn't lying about not fucking her, which is crazy, since she's technically still his woman. Niggas can be so dumb sometimes! Don't they know that when they change outta the blue like that, it's a red flag to the wifey or the girlfriend that they're dipping their dick in some other bitch? You can't go from fucking your woman damn near every day to not touching her for weeks at a time. They end up gettin' caught 'cause their bitches ain't as dumb as they think. Taz oughtta know that shit. His damn ass better be careful.

After we finish eating, we pay the bill and leave. I drop her and her bags off at home before heading to my place.

About an hour later, I'm still about ten minutes from my house when my phone rings. I look at the caller ID, roll my eyes, and let it go to voicemail. No sooner than the ringing stops, it starts again, and this time I answer. "Yeah?"

"You busy?"

"Kind of. What's up?"

"What you getting into later?"

"My bed."

He chuckles. "Sounds good to me. Mind if I join you?"

"Look, Xavier, I don't know what type of chicks you're used to dealing with, but I ain't one of them. I haven't talked to yo' ass in almost a week, then you call me outta the blue, expectin' a hook-up. I'll pass." I suck my teeth with my lips, thinking about all the bags I've gotta lug into my apartment.

"Damn, bay. It's like that? I ain't even been in town since the last time I saw you. I just been busy takin' care of shit, that's all."

"That's fine. You don't gotta do me no favors. If you're busy, stay that way," I tell him, ready to hang up.

He exhales. "I'm sorry, baby, and you're right. I shoulda called you. I've been trying to get everything situated down at my club, and I'm tryin' to find a house. I'm sick and tired of staying in these damn hotels."

Xavier recently moved to Ohio from Chicago. He owns a club in the Windy City, but he left his brother there to run it. Now, he's in the process of opening a second one downtown, a twenty-one and older place called Skye. In the meantime, he keeps having to drive back and forth to make sure everything transitions smoothly. I know what he's saying is true, because I did a background check on that nigga. I ain't one to believe everything I hear! Still, even though I know everything he's saying is legit, I don't care. I don't like to be ignored.

"Yeah, yeah. Tell me anything," I finally say.

"Baby, please let me make it up to you."

"I don't know, Xavier. I'm tired from shopping all day, and I just wanna lie down," I whine as I pull into my designated parking space.

"I promise to make it worth your while," he pleads.

"Fine. What time do you plan on coming by?"

"Now."

"Huh?"

"I'm already here."

I look up and see him sitting in his car across from me, and I can't do anything but laugh. He knew all the time I was gonna give in to his fine ass.

I step out of my truck and grab my purse. "Good. In that case, you can help me carry all these damn bags!"

CHAPTER 11

Inside my apartment, I take a seat on the couch while I wait for Xavier to bring up the rest of my bags like he's some kinda bellhop. A faint smile covers my face; he can be such a gentleman, and that's more than I can say for a lot of the dudes out there.

When he finally drags the last bag up, he sets it down and walks over to stand behind the couch.

I close my eyes, lean my head back, and allow my body to relax when I feel his strong hands massaging my shoulders.

"How was your day?" he asks.

"Pretty good," I moan.

"You look exhausted."

"Trust me, I am."

He walks away and returns a few minutes later. He squats directly in front of me and grabs each of my legs, then removes my shoes one by one and places them beside the couch.

"Stand up," he orders.

I obey.

He releases the belt on my dress, then unbuttons it and pulls it down over my soft shoulders. Once it's around my ankles, he grabs hold of my hand and assists me as I step out of it. A jolt of electricity shoots through my body when his hands touch my shoulders once again. He turns me around and skillfully unclasps my bra. My nipples spring to life as soon as the chilly air hits them, but he quickly warms them with his mouth. A groan escapes my lips, and I get weak in the knees. A trail of soft kisses moves from my breast to my collarbone and straight to my lips. I open my mouth, and when our tongues connect, it takes my breath away.

Using both hands, he slowly slides my panties down around my thighs. I wiggle out of them and kick them across the room. My arms wander up and wrap around his neck, but he pulls away.

"Are you a dirty girl?"

"What?"

"I ran you some bathwater, baby," he says.

I attempt to step away, but he stops me.

"I want you to enjoy your bath, and by the time you get out, I'll have dinner ready."

I say nothing and simply smile and walk away.

The bathwater feels wonderful, and since I have a hair appointment tomorrow, I don't even bother to wrap it up. I rest my head against the bath pillow and sigh. The truth is, I don't know what I'm going to do with Xavier. He's a great guy, but I don't think it will ever work. Shit, truthfully, I don't want it to. Great as he is, I know I can't ever trust him. I've learned the hard way not to trust anybody. I close my eyes and think back on how things used to be with Roger and me, how he used to make me feel. Happy doesn't even describe how I felt when I was around him, and it scares me that I'm catching those same feelings for Xavier.

About an hour later, the bathroom door opens, and in walks Xavier. "How's your bath?"

"It's great. Thank you."

"Are you ready for dinner?"

"Yes. What did you pick up?" I ask.

"Pick up? Naw, baby. You deserve better than takeout after the day you've had. I cooked you something special. You'll see in a minute." He smiles.

"You cooked?" I asked, surprised.

"I'm not retarded, you know. I can cook."

"Yeah right. I still don't believe you." I curl my lips to the side.

"Let me prove it." He opens up a towel, and I stand up and allow him to wrap me in it. He slowly pats my body dry, as if I'm a small child. When all the water is wiped away, he grabs my robe off the hook beside the shower and helps me into it.

I slide my feet into my slippers, and we both head into the kitchen.

My chin drops into my chest when I see what he's been up to while I was soaking. My dining room table is draped with a white tablecloth and decorated with gold ribbons and pretty bows at the end. White plates with matching gold trim are flanked by gold utensils that he must have brought with him. A glass vase sits on the left end of the table, with a dozen pink pearl roses tucked inside, centered between two ivory candles that are the only light source in the room. A medium-sized ice bucket holds a fancy bottle of wine.

I take a seat in the chair he's pulled out for me, still amazed.

He walks away, only to return seconds later with a gold platter in his hand. I shake my head and smile when he places it in the middle of the table; he never ceases to amaze me. Two lobsters sit directly in the middle, surrounded by corn on the cob and a baked potato that's split in half, speckled with salt and pepper and fresh-cut chives. A round dipping bowl is off to the side, filled with creamy butter.

The ice jumbles around in the ice bucket when he reaches inside to grab the chardonnay. After filling up our two flutes, he finally takes a seat in the chair across from me. "Well, what do you think?" he asks as the candlelight gleams in his eyes.

"I think you did a pretty good job. I'm surprised," I answer honestly.

He chuckles. "Why are you surprised?"

"I don't know. Maybe it's because you're different—nothing like all the guys I've run into. Also…oh, never mind." I exhale. I really don't want to have this conversation with him right now—or maybe never.

"Don't shut down on me, Brandy. Just tell me how you feel."

"I'm not shutting down. I just don't have anything else to say," I lie. "Let's just enjoy this wonderful meal you made for us."

He knows I'm lying, but he doesn't push the issue, and I'm glad for that.

We eat in silence, occasionally stealing glances at one another.

My flute is filled twice more before we're done, and I'm full but kind of tipsy. I don't know where his ass learned to cook, but I owe him a big-time tip.

Xavier stands up and grabs our plates and takes them into the kitchen.

I close my eyes and rub circles around my stuffed stomach until I hear him call my name. When I open my eyes, I see him walking toward me with a small plate in his hand. I don't get a good look at what's on top of it till he places it in front of me and pulls up a chair for himself. There are small pieces of what looks like bread on the plate, with some sort of frosting and a strawberry in the middle. It's lightly dusted with powdered sugar, and some kind of caramel-looking sauce is drizzled over the top. "What are these?"

"Strawberry creampuffs. I made them just for you," he says, picking one up.

They look irresistible, and even though I'm super full, I still open my mouth and take a bite. "Oh my God! Those are so good!" I exclaim, still chewing. "How do you make them?" I ask.

"Well, a good chef doesn't give away his secrets, but I'll be happy to make them for you again anytime," he says with a smile. "That way, there'll always be a reason for you to let me stick around." He winks.

"You're so crazy! At least tell me what the creamy filling is."

"Vanilla custard, but it's very hard to make…almost impossible."

"Ha-ha. Very funny."

When he holds up another one, I purposely smear the custard all over his fingers. Instead of letting him wipe it off with a napkin, I lick it off of him teasingly. I suck his fingers down to the knuckle, and I can tell he's feeling me, because a bulge grows in his pants. When I hear him moan, I put a little more into it and begin to lick all around his index finger like it's the best lollipop I ever had in my life.

"You're a nasty girl," he says, his voice husky and full of desire.

"And you like it." I wink at him, get up from the chair, and walk toward my bedroom. As soon as I step through the door, I untie my robe and let it fall to the floor. When I hear him enter behind me, I turn around and face him, butt-ass naked. There ain't no shame in my game, and I know my body's tight.

"Lie down on your stomach and close your eyes," he commands.

I crawl across the bed slowly, sticking my butt out. I hear the sound of liquid being poured before I feel his warm touch. He slowly rubs small circles all over my back. When I feel his strong hands on my shoulders, it seems as if all the tension is leaving my body, and I damn near have an orgasm when they come in contact with my plump ass. His warm breath blows on the lower part of my back as he gently applies pressure to my butt cheeks. Slowly, he moves down my legs and eventually to my feet. When he's done with both my feet, he works his way back up to my butt, then spreads my cheeks apart. A whimper escapes my lips when I feel his tongue brush against the crack of my ass.

He slides it up and down before dipping his stiff tongue into the hole, all while pushing my ass back so he can go deeper. When he forces his entire tongue inside and begins to wiggle it around, I grip the sheets, and my eyes roll in the back of my head. I've had a lot of sex before, but no one has ever put his mouth on my ass crack. That's just one thing that separates him from everybody else, and I absolutely love it!

"Get up. I want you to sit on my face," he says, then lies down on his back.

He motions for me to come to him and assists me in straddling his face. He parts my pussy lips with two fingers, then dives right in. My back arches as I allow him to fuck me with his tongue, and before long, I'm bouncing up and down on it like it's his dick. I tighten my muscles around his tongue and squeeze and lower myself down farther. It feels so good, and I damn near lose my mind when he starts to massage my ass cheeks while eating my pussy; this man sure knows how to please a woman. I haven't sucked a dick since Roger, but the way he's working me over, I owe him an oral pleasure.

While his tongue's still inside me, I maneuver my body so we end up in a sixty-nine position. I lose track of what I'm doing and lay my head on his leg when I feel his mouth grab hold of my clit and apply pressure. I bite down on my bottom lip and grind on him gently. I involuntarily bounce up and down as soon as his tongue enters my love hole again. I can't stay focused while he's doing that, so I hop up and move down till I'm standing between his legs. Since he's still dressed, I unhook the buckle of his True Religion jeans and push them down around his thighs with his help. I do the same thing with his briefs, then engulf his dick with my warm mouth.

"Damn, baby," I hear him say when I pull it out of my mouth and begin nibbling on the head.

He pulls his shirt off and rest on his elbows, waiting to see my handiwork. I suck and lick all around his dick before jacking him off with both his balls in my mouth. When I start to hum, a look of pure ecstasy comes over his face.

"You like that, don't you?" I ask before trying to swallow it whole.

Relaxing my throat muscles, I take him all the way in, in one quick motion. He guides my head with his hands and moves his hips while he fucks my warm mouth. In no time, I've got him cumming like there's no tomorrow. Like a pro, I take everything he gives me, hungrily swallowing every drop.

By the time I'm done, he's rock hard again, lying back on the bed and looking like he's just ran a marathon.

"Don't tell me you tired." I smirk.

"Naw. I'm just getting ready to wear yo' ass out!" He kicks his pants and underwear onto the floor at the foot of the bed.

"Well then, come on daddy. I'm looking forward to it," I say, climbing on top of him.

Using my hand, I guide his hard penis inside of me and begin to bounce up and down on it the same way I bounced on his tongue not too long ago. The only difference is that my pussy is filled to capacity with the thick piece of chocolate that I can't get enough of. With my right hand, I place one of my breasts in my own mouth. I grind into him roughly, bringing myself to my first orgasm. My body hasn't completely stop shaking before he flips me over onto my back and tries to push his shit into my stomach. It hurts so good every time his pelvis connects with mine. With each thrust, he's got my titties bouncing all over the place, and it feels so good when he begins to use them as leverage to fuck me harder.

"Aw, fuck!" I cry. My body is feeling something I've never felt before. "Right there, baby! Don't stop. God, please don't stop! Keep hitting that spot!"

This really warm feeling takes over my body and grows stronger by the second. It consumes me, getting hotter and hotter. I can't explain the feeling, but I damn sure love it. I'm scared but excited at the same time. My heart pounds in my chest, and my body tenses up everywhere, while my breath catches in my throat. Xavier keeps doing what I asked, hitting that spot repeatedly. A volt of energy shoots from my brain down to my toes, and before I know what's happening, a gush of my juices spews out all over him. I scream out as I continue to release everything in me.

"Damn, baby! You okay?" Xavier asks, but I'm too spent to even answer.

The covers are soaking wet, but I don't care. All I want to do is lie here and rest, and my body is still tingling. I've never cum so hard in my life, and it felt so damn good.

Xavier scoots closer and wraps his arms around me tightly, and before I know it, I've drifted off to sleep.

* * *

2003...

It's been almost a week since Pitch threw me up here in this attic, with nothing to eat. All that's up here is a small rollaway bed and a bucket, which is supposed to serve as a toilet till I'm allowed to go downstairs again—till I "Learn not to be an ungrateful bitch," as my daddy so lovingly put it. It stinks so bad up here, and there are flies everywhere because they're attracted to the feces in the bucket. I've been freezing every night, because he didn't bother to give me a blanket or anything to cover up with. Even worse, I'm completely naked, because he brought me right up here the minute he was finished raping me the day I refused to be his whore.

A couple days ago, he brought up a huge plate of food from some New Year's party he was throwing downstairs without me. He set it right in front of me and told me that if I so much as looked in the direction of the plate, he'd break my fucking neck. My stomach did all types of somersaults when I smelled that food, and I wanted so bad to just have one taste, but I knew better. Taking his threat seriously, I just sat there with my eyes fixed on the ceiling, praying that he wouldn't accuse me of looking at the food and beat me within an inch of my life.

Cachet

My bruises haven't had a chance to heal from my first assault, because he comes up daily just to smack me around. My body is sore all over, and I really don't know how much more I can take.

To make matters worse, I started my period yesterday. Since I don't have no pads or tampons or nothing, I just have to let blood run down my leg. Not only is it disgusting, but it's also humiliating. I feel like a damn animal. Even that doesn't stop my daddy from fucking me two or three times a day. He says he's just trying to teach me a lesson, but that shit's nasty, no matter what he's trying to teach.

Even if he doesn't want to bring me any feminine hygiene products, he needs to bring up something, anything for me to eat. If I don't get something soon, I'm going to die up here for sure. It's crazy, but I feel the same way now, that I used to feel when I lived with my sorry excuse for a mother. So many days, I lay in my room starving, so hungry that I was sure I was going to die at any moment.

I've gotta wonder what it is about me that makes people treat me this way, why they all want to hurt me so bad. I don't understand why I'm not entitled to a normal life or what I could have possibly done so wrong in thirteen years of life that I deserve to be treated like garbage.

When I hear someone lower the attic stairs, I hold my breath. I know it's Pitch, coming up to beat or rape me again, but I'm relieved when I see Trixie, carrying a small bowl and a bottle of water.

"Pitch won't be back for a few hours, so eat up. You'll need your energy," she tells me.

I look down at the bowl, full of rice, three chicken wings, and a biscuit—the best-looking meal I've ever seen in my life, even if it is kind of cold.

"How are you, Baby Doll?" she asks, calling me by the pet name she gave me. Her face is covered with a worried expression, like she knows how bad it really is but can't do anything about it.

"I'm okay, I guess. I just really want to get out of here," I tell her between bites.

"You'll be out sooner than you think. Trust me."

"Why is he doing this to me, Trixie?"

"It's a long story, Baby Doll, but the truth is, your father has been a pimp for as long as I've known him. As a matter of fact, I used to work for him years ago. Now, he leaves it up to me to get the new girls ready to go out and work the track."

"So you knew he was gonna put me out on the track way before he said something to me about it?" I ask, amazed and pissed at the same time. She's been like a mother to me, and I'm sick and tired of mother figures screwing me over—first my own, and now her.

She doesn't answer and only drops her eyes in shame.

"Are you tellin' me all that bonding I thought we were doing was just you getting me ready to be a ho?" Tears spill down my face as I ask the question, and if I even have a heart left, it shatters all over again. For all this time, I thought Trixie really cared about me, but she was just grooming me to do my daddy's dirty business. As starved as I am, I almost lose my appetite. Again I'm reminded that nobody loves me.

"In the beginning, I was just trying to work the plan, but as time went on, I grew to love you like a daughter. I wanted to help you that day in the room, but there was nothing I could do. I don't want you to have to do this. Hell, I even told him I'll go back out and work if he'd just keep you outta the streets," she tells me sympathetically. "He told me to forget that and that I'd better mind my own damn business, and then he gave me this." She pulls her hair out of her face and shows me a black eye. It's starting to heal, but I can still see it.

"If he's so awful, why don't you leave?"

"I only stay because I don't have anywhere else to go. I'm from Trinidad, and if INS catches me, I'll be deported. I'm here illegally, Brandy, and I've got no family here or there. I've really got no choice but to do what your father says. Pitch has taken care of me over the years, and even though I've had to do some crazy things, it's a whole lot better than being back home." She wipes her eyes with the back of her hand and takes a seat beside me. "See, in my country, women and children are sold as sex slaves every day, and there's nothing we can do about it. My mother and father were killed when I was seven, and my sister and I were sold right after that. I haven't seen her since. I ended up in the United States and met Pitch when I was sixteen. Yes, he made me sell my body the same way the sex traffickers did, but at least I still got to live. Back home, women sell their bodies for their entire lives for nothing more than a little food and water. There's no shopping, no friends, no being normal—only going from owner to owner. I felt like a slave there, but Pitch showed me a way out." By now, her face is soaking wet with tears.

"I disagree, Trixie. Bad as it is where you came from, this is no way to live either. I don't wanna live if it's gotta be this way."

"I don't want you to live like this either, Baby Doll. That's why I'm gonna get you outta here."

"But how? What are you talking about, Trixie?" I ask, puzzled. "I'm afraid he'll kill us both if we try."

"I don't care. We have to try. You deserve to be free from this life. You're young, and you have so many years ahead of you. You won't be able to live your life like you deserve as long as you're stuck here, under your daddy's control." She stands up and hands me a jogging outfit and a pad.

I get dressed quickly, and it feels so good to put on clothes again.

Next, she hands me a wad of money.

"What's this for?" I ask, looking at what must be a few thousand dollars.

"Baby Doll, it's for you to get away. It should be enough to last you a while. I've been pinching money off the top for the past year just so I could get you away from here. I was gonna give it to you and tell you to get out before Pitch told you about the track, but he tricked me and did it a week early."

"What about you? Why don't you come with me? We can live together or something. I can get a job, and we can tell everybody you're my mother," I beg, hoping she'll comply. "I don't wanna be out in the big world all alone, Trixie. Please come with me," I plead.

"Listen here, Baby Doll. You're gonna be okay. Do you hear me? You're a strong girl, and you can do anything you put your mind you. You just gotta want to do it." She leads me toward the stairs and helps me down.

"But what about my father? He's gonna freak when he sees that I've escaped, and I'm afraid he'll take it out on you."

"Don't you worry about him. I'll just tell Pitch you got out somehow."

But when we round the corner, we run smack dab into none other than the devil himself, and our eyes grow as wide as saucers as we realize he's been listening the whole time.

"So, not only have you been stealing from me, but you've also had plans on letting my new ho go, huh?" he asks Trixie with a menacing look in his eyes.

I'm so scared I can't hold my bladder and promptly piss all over myself, soaking the fleece of the outfit she gave me.

* * *

"I'm sorry, Daddy! Please don't hurt me. I'm so sorry. No! Stop!" I scream out, kicking and screaming.

"Brandy? Brandy, baby wake up. It's all right, sweetheart. You're safe with me."

I open my eyes and through my tears see Xavier staring at me.

"Are you okay?" he asks with concern in his eyes.

"Everything is fine. It was just a bad dream," I say, wiping my tears away.

"Sounds more like a fucking nightmare. You've been tossing and turning for the past few hours. I wanted to wake you up, but I was scared to touch you."

"Really? I'm sorry. It's nothing really. Don't worry about it."

"Are you sure? It seemed so…real," he pushes, trying to pull me closer.

"I said it's nothing, damn it! It was only a dream, Xavier," I snap, jerking away from. "What's your fucking problem anyway? If I say it was only a bad dream, then that's all the fuck it was! Quit giving me the damn third degree and listen to what I'm telling you. Why are you all in my damn business anyway?"

"Well excuse the fuck outta me." He jumps up from the bed and grabs his clothes from the floor, then makes his way to the bathroom. A minute later, he emerges, fully dressed. "Catch you later, I guess," he says as he stomps toward my bedroom door.

"Bye!" I yell at his back.

He stops at the door and turns around in a hurry. "Look, I don't know what the fuck your problem is, but I'm not one of these lames you usually deal with. I'ma let you slide with that slick shit because of that so-called bad dream you had that had you all kicking the hell outta me like some Bruce Lee shit, but the next time you talk to me like that, I'm gonna hafta put your ass in its place. You will give me the same respect I give you, or we're gonna have a problem. I'm trying with you, Brandy, but you make it so hard, being the way you are. I'll tell you what. You call me when you're ready to talk and not a minute sooner. If you don't ever speak to me again, it was fun while it lasted, baby." With that, he turns and walks out, and I hear the front door slam behind him.

I don't know who the fuck he thinks he is, because I don't kiss nobody's ass, no matter how fine they are. As far as I'm concerned, he can leave and never come back. I don't give a damn. Xavier ain't the only nigga in the world who gives good dick, so fuck him!

CHAPTER 12

On the morning when we're scheduled to leave for Vegas, I jump out of bed and check my bags to make sure I packed everything.

When Osha calls to let me know she's pulling up in front of my apartment, I carefully place the shoulder strap of my Louis Vuitton overnight bag over my head so I don't mess up my hair. I make my way over to the door, where my two matching suitcases are already waiting. All I have to do is fasten the strap of my Marc Jacobs tote on top of the handle, and I'm on my way. The elevator ride is a quick one with no stops or other riders to bother me, and I'm in the lobby in no time.

Outside, Osha's Escalade is double-parked in the front of the building. She climbs out when she notices me, and we both stuff my belongings into the truck, then head to the airport.

The plane ride takes about four hours, and the time flies by as we laugh and joke, especially about the other passengers.

We get off the plane in Vegas and head to the baggage claim. After retrieving our luggage, we look around and notice a guy in a black suit and matching hat, holding a cardboard sign with our names written on it. He tells us he's our personal chauffeur and says we should follow him. We're shocked when he opens the door of a pearl-white Maybach and gestures for us to enter.

The drive takes about thirty minutes, and as soon as we pull up, the concierge greets us in the front of the hotel. She's a middle-aged white woman, dressed in a gray skirt and matching blazer with the MGM Grand logo on the front. She's wearing a warm smile, but I can hardly see it behind that ridiculously thick coat of makeup she painted on.

With keycards in hand, we make our way up to our designated floor. We slide the keycard through the slot and open the door when the lock clicks open and the green light comes on. My jaw drops at the sight of what will be our deluxe living quarters for the next week.

The entire suite is beautiful and looks even better than it did in the pictures I saw in the brochures and on the Internet. We have an outdoor deck and our own personal pool, with an amazing view. Both bedrooms are elegant, and the attached bathrooms have thirty-two-inch TVs in front of the bathtubs. The small, clear television inside the mirror is too damn cute; I can't even believe someone thought of that. The room is amazing, and I'm looking forward to whatever else the hotel has to offer.

After the personal butler delivers some light cuisine to our room, we head down to the casino to try our luck. We decide our luck will be better if we split up, and I end up winning about three grand on the slot machines. An older gentleman beside me keeps cramming his quarters in there and hitting the jackpot. I figure he's got about $15,000 worth of coins, but he's not ready to give up and doesn't budge from his chair. I'm sure he thinks it's a lucky machine or something, but the second his ass leaves that seat, mine's sure as hell gonna replace it, 'cause that ol' dude's got some kind of muthafuckin' luck at that particular slot machine, and I want a piece of that jackpot.

Another hour goes by, and I begin to get frustrated 'cause he won't move his wrinkly ass out of the chair. I'm pissed because I've gone from $3,000 to about $500. I gather up my things and head back upstairs. On top of everything else, I've grown bored with gambling for the day, and it ain't no fun if you ain't winnin'.

As I stand in front of the elevator, waiting to ride up to our floor, I wonder where Osha is since I haven't seen or heard her since we stepped into the casino.

"Brandy!"

I turn and see ol' girl walking toward me with a Kool-Aid grin on her face. "What's up, girl?" I ask.

"Girl, I met someone already, and he's so fine!"

Damn! She works fast. I thought I was going to have to pump her up to do the damn thang, but she's doing fine on her own. "Um, okay. When did this happen? We only been here a couple hours."

"I was playing blackjack when he walked his fine ass over and asked me for my name. We just started talking like we've known each other forever. Brandy, he's so sexy!" she exclaims, all excited and shit.

"Where is he?" I look around, wanting to see Mr. Sexy for myself.

"He went to get his brother. Tonight's their last night here, and he invited me to dinner, but I told him I couldn't let you eat alone. He suggested we make a double-date of it, and I told him I was sure you'd be cool with it. Girl, I'm sure his brother is as fine as he is! I hope you don't mind, but I also told him it's cool if they wanna come up to our room after dinner and chill with us, maybe sit by the pool or something."

My neck jerks back, and I look at her, annoyed. "Why would you do that? We don't know these dudes, Osha." I don't know what the fuck she's thinking, inviting some random-ass dudes back to where we're gonna be resting our heads for the next week.

"Oh. Sorry. I didn't think it would be a problem. We don't have any plans for tonight, and it is a ladies' getaway, right?"

"Yeah, you're right. It's cool. We can do that. Do you know which restaurant we're going to?"

"No, but it's casual everywhere in here, so we good. We exchanged cell numbers, and I told him I'll call him in a minute to make sure everything's all set."

Damn! She ain't even playing. I guess she is ready to loosen up and take her mind of Taz.

We both catch the elevator up, and I head into my bedroom so I can find something to wear to dinner. A few minutes later, Osha knocks on my door and tells me we have reservations for 10:30. I glance at the clock and see that it's only 9:00, so I've got enough time to do what I need to do. Osha's ass is tripping, but I'm not mad; it makes it easier to kill two birds with one stone. Not only am I gonna get some dick, but I'm also gonna set Osha's ass up all in one night. I just hope this nigga's brother is cute and well endowed in the pocket and the pants.

After my shower, I decide I want to wear something simple and sexy at the same time. I know the beige Hervé Léger bandage dress hugs my body, showing off every curve. It has a square neckline that sits nice against my perky breast. I comb my wrap out and put my black onyx David Yurman earrings in my ears, then clasp on the matching necklace and bracelet. The small Prada clutch has just enough room for my lip gloss, debit card, and keycard. I slip my feet into a pair of beige and black patent-leather Christian Louboutin pumps, then step out, dressed to impress.

When I see Osha, I'm shocked, because she actually looks like a grown woman. "Osha, is that you?" I ask, being silly.

She bursts out laughing, then strikes a pose for me like she's in the pages of *Vogue*. "You like?"

"Girl, you look really pretty," I say, telling her the truth.

I can tell she's really feeling herself, and even though I picked out all of her wardrobe, she's making it work. She's got hella cleavage in her soft pink Ali Ro ballerina dress. The crossover V-neck stops just above the black sash tied around her waist, and the ruffles that bloom below it, down to her mid thigh, make her look deliciously thicker than she really is. Her feet are in black Dior platform pumps with a cute little tassel on the front. I can't believe she actually wore those shoes, because it was like pulling teeth to get her to buy them, since she swore they're ugly. Her hair is still in her signature style, but it looks cute with the outfit she's rocking.

"Can you give me a hand with this?" she asks, handing me her pearl David Yurman necklace; she's already wearing the matching earrings and bracelet. "You ready to go?" she asks as she grabs her clutch.

"Yep."

Downstairs, Osha tells the *maître d'* at Tom Colicchio's Craftsteak, "It's under Chad," and we are promptly escorted to our table.

Two men stand as we approach. One is so damn fine that my pussy begins to pulsate. He resembles a slightly darker version of Michael Jai White, with the body to match. The other guy isn't ugly, but he's not my style; I'm praying like hell he's the one Osha plans to hook up with. He's plain-looking, with huge lips that don't seem to fit the rest of his face. When the other guy, Mr. Sexy, pulls Osha in for a quick hug and kiss on the cheek and reaches out to shake my hand, I'm utterly disappointed.

"Welcome. My name is Chad, and this is my brother, Chino." He smiles, and I notice that he even has a small gap in the middle of his teeth like Michael.

"Hello, Chad and Chino. My name is Brandy," I say, my eyes never leaving Chad's.

"Hi, Chino. I'm Osha," she says, clearing her throat, as if she can feel the instant connection between me and her date.

Oh fuckin' well! I know for a fact I'm gonna fuck him tonight, and I don't care what Osha has in mind.

The waiter takes our order, and we make small talk while we await our food, trying to get to know each other a bit more. Chino's pretty cool and keeps us all laughing with all the silly things he says. Chad cracks a few jokes here and there, but I can tell he's the more serious of the two.

I really don't say much, since I'm just trying to feel everybody out, but Osha runs her mouth like she's got oral diarrhea or some shit. She keeps going on and on about everything under the sun, giving perfect strangers way too much information. There's no need for them to know she's got three kids and a man at home. We're in Vegas, and last time I checked, what goes on here is supposed to stay here, and vice versa. Nevertheless, she insists on telling Chad her whole damn life story, and I can tell he's not even feeling that at all. I just shake my head and laugh to myself, because ol' girl ain't got a clue. *I don't know how in the world she managed to snag Taz, because she's boring the shit outta these guys.*

Dinner goes pretty well, though, considering that Osha keeps on running her mouth, especially after a few glasses of wine. She throws them bitches back like she's some kind of alcoholic.

When the bill comes, almost $700, Chad grabs it and pays it without a second thought, while Chino doesn't even acknowledge that it's on the table. Now I know who has all the money, the looks, and the charm—and probably the biggest dick. I didn't have no plans to fuck with Chino anyway, but that just sealed the deal. If there's one thing I can't stand, it's a broke-ass man.

"Do you guys wanna go to our room and get in the pool?" I invite, fixating my hungry eyes on Chad.

"Sure. We'll just go to our room and get our trunks, then meet back up with you ladies," he replies.

Osha and I take the elevator up to our floor and make our way into the room. She's holding up pretty well so far, but I know she'll succumb to her drunken state before long, and I can't fucking wait for her to pass the fuck out. "Girrrrl, ain't he fine?" she slurs.

"Yeah, he cool," I say, but deep down I want to scream, *"Hell yeah, bitch!"*

"What you think about Chino?"

"He's not really my type, but he's cool too, I guess."

"He's funny as hell! I swear, he had me cracking up with his silly ass!"

"Yeah, me too. Anyway, we better get ready. They'll be here soon."

Twenty minutes later, a knock comes at the door, and I open it to find Chad and Chino standing behind it. Their jaws drop at the sight of me in my metallic gold, two-piece La Perla. The bikini top puts my boobs on display and shows just enough cleavage, while the skimpy bottom barely covers my plump cheeks, spilling out from each side.

"It took y'all long enough," I tease, turning around to give the brothers an eyeful of what one of them is about to get.

"My fault. We lost our room key, so we had to go down and get a new one," Chino says, staring at me lustfully.

I don't pay his ass any mind. It's Chad I want, and it's Chad I'm going to get. "Oh. Sorry to hear that. You guys can follow me. Osha isn't ready yet."

When we walk outside, the view is even better than I expected. There are neon and flashing lights everywhere I look, and so much is going on all around and below us. Clearly, the city never sleeps, and I can see why people love to come here so much. I decide then and there to make it my business to visit Vegas again—soon and often.

Both men take off their shirts and climb into the pool. I lick my lips and take in the sight before me: I'm talking abs for days! I hand them each a flute of champagne, then sit my fine ass on one of the lounge chairs to stir up a little more small talk.

Before long, Osha stumbles in, dressed in a chocolate-brown one-piece with a plunge down to her belly button. The thin straps that tie around her neck look like they are stretched to the max, trying to hold those big-ass jugs. She's tipsy, but I don't know how tipsy. "Hey! I thought I heard the door." She smiles and climbs into the water slowly. "Whew! It's kind of cold in here."

"I poured you a drink," I say, handing her the glass I mixed especially for her.

Without a thought, she gulps it down and hands the empty

glass back to me.

"Quit sitting over there looking pretty and come join us," Chino says before splashing a bunch of water on me.

"Stop! I don't want to get my hair wet!" I scream, trying to cover my head with my hands. When I put my hands down, I see him climbing out of the water and walking toward me. I smile and scoot back as far as I can on the lounge chair, staring into his dark eyes. Now that he's up close and personal, I realize he doesn't look that bad, but I figure that might be the champagne talking.

Chino's skin is deep walnut, and he has thick eyebrows and a full, sloped nose. Large lips with a hint of pink sit at the bottom of his face, framed by a well-trimmed goatee. I know there ain't no way in the world that nigga don't eat pussy like a pro, and if I didn't have my sights set on his brother, I'd have to test them bad boys out.

"Put me down!" I yell when he picks me and walks toward the water.

I close my eyes, sure he's about to throw me in the water at any moment, but instead he walks slowly into the pool with me. My body shivers as it adjusts to the cool temperature. I hear him laughing and open my eyes to see what's so funny.

"Did you think I was really gonna throw you in?" he smiles.

"Yes!" I yell, throwing water in his face. I then turn around and swim away so he can't catch me.

Chad grabs Osha quickly and dunks her in the water. The look on her face is priceless. This starts an all-out water fight, and I realize I'm actually having fun.

A few moments later, I excuse myself to go to the bathroom and leave the three of them in the water. Inside, I brush my hair into a tighter ponytail and apply more lip gloss. The small beads of water on my body chill me in the air-conditioned room. I'm shocked when I open the bathroom door and find Chad standing there. "Damn! You scared me."

"Sorry. Should I go?" he asks seductively.

"No. You can stay in here with me as long as you want," I flirt.

"Good. See, your girl's passed out cold out there, and I'm feelin' kinda lonely. Just give me a minute to get rid of Chino, and I'll be back."

"Okay."

In the living room, I find the sliding door closed and Osha out cold on the couch. I don't see Chino anywhere. I help Osha up into her room so she won't be on the couch when Chad returns. I'm counting on her being out for the rest of the night, considering how many drinks she's had, combined with the sleeping pills I crushed up in her champagne. I struggle to peel the wet swimming suit off her while she lies unconscious on the bed. Once she's out of her soaked suit, I pull the covers up to her neck, turn out the lights, and close the door.

I grab all my stuff and step into the steaming shower, hoping I'll be finished before Chad drags his fine ass back here. I remove my hair from the ponytail holder and massage the Victoria's Secret So Sexy shampoo into my scalp, as I refuse to let that chlorine sit in my hair. I follow with conditioner, wash up, and step out, grabbing one of the thick white towels to dry myself. I prance back into my bedroom and pull out the drawer that holds my night clothes. Even though I know I'm only gonna be wearing it for a little while, I want to show Chad he's dealing with a bad bitch. By the end of the night, the only thoughts he'll be having about Osha is that she's got a fine-ass friend who rocked his world.

Twenty minutes later, I strut to the door slowly when I hear a slight knock. I open it to find Chad standing there, sexy as ever. Instinctively, I bite down on the corner of my lip when he smiles. *Damn, this man is fine!* Gone are the swimming trunks, and he's now dressed in a pair of khaki cargo shorts and a red and blue Ralph Lauren polo shirt that hugs his muscles ever so gently. I step out of the way to let him enter, and when he does, he leaves a trail of the Clive Christian cologne behind him, a scent I adore.

After closing and locking the door, I grab hold of his hand and guide him up the stairs and into my bedroom.

He takes a seat on the bed and kicks off his high-top Polo shoes and places them beside my bed. "Damn." He licks his full lips. "You sexy as hell."

"Am I?"

"Hell yeah! You know I wanted you from the first time I saw you, right?"

"I felt the same way, but are we gonna talk or fuck?" I ask, getting right to the point.

In no time, he's standing before me with nothing on. His chest is so chiseled and his arms are so big that they barely sit right at his sides. His thick, muscular thighs and toned calves are a sight to see. The best part is the fat chunk of solid meat dangling between his legs. I know the muthafucka's gotta be straight from Africa with a dick that big. I'm almost scared to allow him to put the monster in me—almost.

He grabs me around my waist, picks me up, and lays me back on the bed. I moan when I feel him nibbling on my nipple that's clearly visible through my sheer black mesh baby doll dress. I rub my hands through the small curls on top of his head as I arch my back to allow him better access. He makes a trail of soft kisses from my nipple down to my stomach, stopping at my inner thigh. His pink tongue licks the outside of my panties; I don't think it's humanly possible for my pussy to get any wetter. He comes back up and kisses my lips as gently as he can, but I grab the back of his head to show him I'm not trying to make love. All I wanna do is fuck, and I don't got time for that take-yo'-time shit.

I guess he finally understands that I just wanna get to it, because he grabs my dress, ripping it into. My thong is next to go, and now I'm lying here just as naked as he is. I have to catch myself from flipping out on his ass, because that damn lingerie was almost $300, but those thoughts disappear when I remember that Taz paid for that shit anyway. I forget about it even more when he buries his face in my pussy and devours it like it's his last supper. I grind on his face while holding his head in place with my hands. I figure he must be enjoying it, because he's making more noise than I am. Even though I think that's weird as hell, I don't say a word.

"Fuck me!" I demand after ten minutes of oral stimulation.

He stands up and clumsily rolls the condom on his big dick; I almost wonder if it's the first time he's ever used one because he seems so awkward with it. When he finally has it on all the way on, stretched to the max, he grabs my legs and yanks me roughly down to the edge of the bed. I don't mind, because I'm ready to get some of that dick. Before he has the chance to do it, I grab hold of his shaft and guide him slowly into my tight hole; I'm scared if he tried it himself, he might rip me in two. Little by little, he enters me, and I try to adjust to his large size. I ain't gonna front: That shit hurts like a muthafucka! I steady my breathing and try to be a big girl about it, but with a dick that size, there ain't no easy way.

Before he's even all the way in, he begins to hump me like a fucking rabbit, going so fast that I can't possibly enjoy it because it hurts so damn bad. He starts moaning and growling like a fuckin' animal. Meanwhile, I'm trying my best to slow him down a bit, because I can feel him all up in my insides, and it ain't in a good way.

"Aw, shit!" he yells as he continues to bang into my body like a damn jackhammer.

"Wait a minute, Chad. You're—" I attempt to tell him, but I'm rendered speechless by what I hear next.

"Oh…fuck! I'm cumming! Baby, I'm cumming! Awwwww, damn!" He pumps faster and faster until every bit of cum drains from his body.

When he pulls out, I just lie on the bed in awe. I can't believe that sexy-ass nigga was such a waste of my fucking time. I thought I was gonna be riding that big muthafucka all night, but ten minutes later, his minute-man ass is all done. Not only was it a complete waste of time, but my pussy's sore as hell from him ramming his shit in me so roughly.

I could've had a V8.

"Look, I gotta go. Our plane's leaving in a few hours, and I gotta get back to my room and pack my stuff."

His hit-it-and-quit-it words are music to my ears, because I don't want to even look at his sorry, selfish ass.

He reaches into the pocket of his shorts and hands me ten $100 bills like I'm some kinda ho. "Sorry about your dress. I'm sure this'll cover it."

"It's cool…and this is fine," I say. I guess he's trying to make me feel better about his fucking and fleeing, but he doesn't know I really don't give two shits.

"Mind if I use your restroom to clean up a little real quick before I go?"

"Nope. Go ahead."

As soon as I hear the faucet turn on in the bathroom, I reach into that same pocket of his shorts and see that it's full of money. I peel off ten more $100 bills and his American Express credit card and place it all under my pillow for safekeeping. By the time he comes back out and begins to get dressed, I'm lying on the bed, pretending I'm tired.

"I had a great time. Can I call you?"

"Yeah, it was good, but I don't think calling's a good idea. I mean, I've kinda got a boyfriend and all," I lie.

"It's cool. Just take my number and call me whenever you get some free time." He hands me a card that reads, "The Tasty Kitten. Chad Taylor, Owner."

Frankly, I'm shocked. I knew the nigga has money, but I didn't know he's got it like that. I just finish fucking the owner of one of the largest chains of strip clubs in the world, and I didn't even know it. I guess if I'd have taken the time to ask him about himself, I would've known that. It's cool, though, because by the time it's all said and done, I'll milk the shit out of him, big dick and all.

"I sure will. I hope you guys have a safe trip." I give him a quick hug, and he's out the door.

Back inside the bedroom, I run a bubble bath. I make it as hot as I can to soak my kitty, which is sore as hell. As I lie inside the tub watching *Married with Children*, my mind drifts to Xavier. I haven't spoken to him in a few days, and truthfully, I kind of miss him. I'm not about to call him, though, because I'll be damned if he thinks he can talk to me any kind of way. I'm a top-notch bitch, and he's lucky I even gave his ass the time of day. There was no need for him to get all emotional on a bitch. After a while, I push him to the back of my mind. I've got more important things to think about, and it starts with getting Osha out of my damn way.

CHAPTER 13

It's our last day in Vegas, and so far I've had a blast! I've won about twenty-two grand playing craps, and that baffles me, since I've never shot dice before in my life. Osha said something about it being beginner's luck, so I'm glad I quit while I was ahead. She was kind of salty about my winnings because she lost about ten stacks and couldn't win it back for shit. Her attitude changed a little after that, and she started acting all sad and depressed, talking about Taz was going to be mad at her because he only gave her $15,000 to spend, and she took more money out of the ATM than she was supposed to. That fucked me up, because he gave me $25,000 to spend, and I ain't even his main bitch! I ain't mad at him, but if I was his main and he tried to put a cap on my spending, he'd sure as hell get his feelings hurt.

Speaking of Taz, he's called a few times to check up on me. I either ignore the call or keep the conversation short and sweet. When I do pick up, I just listen for a minute and then tell him I've gotta go and that I'll see him when I get back. You'd think he'd take the hint and wait till I get back, but the very next day, he just calls again, and I tell him the same damn thing. The more I put him off, the more he gets a little attitude in his voice, but I ain't his woman—at least not yet. Nothing in the rule book says I gotta carry on a thirty-minute conversation with his ass while I'm on vacation. We don't talk on the phone like that when I'm home, so I can't see no point in doing it now. I'm sure he's just scared that I've been giving this pussy away, but after that fiasco with Chad, I'm kinda scared too. My shit still hurts from his rough ass. What a waste of a good dick!

I ask Osha if she's spoken to her man, and she says he hasn't answered any of her numerous calls. "He's probably laid up with his new bitch and don't got no time to talk to me," she says. "The kids have been staying with Zema and Dan, so I guess he figures he's free to do whatever the hell or whoever the hell he wants till we get back."

I roll my eyes and laugh, telling her she's just tripping and assuring her that Taz loves her.

She stares at me stone-faced and doesn't so much as smile; I guess she don't find a damn thing funny about it.

Anywho, since Chad and Chino left and she started losing money, she's been spending most of her time holed up in her room like a fucking hermit or something. All she does is lie in bed and watch TV or read from that stupid-ass Kindle she brought with her. When I first saw her pull that shit out of her bag, you should've seen the look on my face. I wanted to snatch that bitch and toss it off the balcony. I mean, who the fuck brings books on a trip to Vegas anyway? A fuckin' loser, that's who! Don't get me wrong: I love to read, and I actually have one myself, but I'd never bring an e-reader to Vegas.

As the days go on, it seems like she's getting more and more depressed. Sad thing is, if it's because of Taz, she ain't seen nothing yet.

I, on the other hand, have done so much in these past few days that I'm sad it's my last day here. I'm gonna have to come back soon, and maybe I can get Taz to bring me next time. They have this CSI-type thing here where you're the investigator and you have to help solve one of three crimes, and that shit's fun as hell! When I got there, I was handed a clipboard and sent on my way. I got to view the crime scene and look over the fake dead body for clues. There are about fifteen lab stations that are used to run tests on all the crime scene clues. There are videos of witnesses and a bunch of suspects but only one killer. The problem is that you have to actually figure out who the killer is in so little time. I now know that a crime scene investigator's job isn't easy, because that shit stumped me for a minute. I ended up figuring it out in the end and received a certificate of completion.

David Copperfield does a show at the hotel too, and I bought a ticket since I was bored that day. I was kind of worried that the show might be kind of weak, since I haven't heard anything about him in years, but it was quite the opposite. That magic man is amazing! I had a front-row seat, so I didn't miss anything. He made two chicks disappear into thin air! One second they were standing there, and in the next, they were gone. I still don't know how or what he did or where those chicks went, but when he was done, the crowd went wild, and I screaming and clapping right along with them.

Two days ago, I saw lions at the lion habitat. Trust me when I tell you it was a sight to see! I couldn't take my eyes off the mane of the male. I've never been to the zoo before, so it was a whole new experience for me. They were walking around behind this huge glass, and two trainers went inside to play with the females, tossing a large bone back and forth between them. Even though they're animals, they seemed to be having fun. It was like in a mini African safari. I was amazed and am glad I stopped to check it out.

Other than doing that, most of my days were spent outside by the pool. If I wasn't in the water, I was sitting in one of the lounge chairs, sipping on some sort of mixed drink. A few dudes tried to holla, but I shut all they asses down real quick because they looked broke as hell, and you know I don't got time for that.

I almost died laughing at the look on this older gentleman's face when I told him he couldn't even afford to smell my pussy. His ass walked away real quick in that fake, tacky-ass Burberry khaki suit. Not only was he dead wrong for rocking the matching hat, but his shirt was tucked in tight as hell around that big-ass gut. Shit, it looked like it was hard for him to breathe. The worst part was that he was wearing a pair of K-Swiss, and I'm not even sure they still make that shit.

I quickly grew tired of doing everything by myself because of Osha's pouty ass sitting in the room like a lump on a log. I tried to cheer her up by taking her to different clubs each night, but she wasn't having it. She shot down every idea I threw her way and had more excuses than a nigga on parole. I don't even see why the hell she came if she was gonna hole up in the room every fucking day. She only comes out of the room to eat, barely every couple of hours. I've been a little worried that she might kill herself or something, the way she's been moping around, looking like an abused puppy and shit. That funk she's in is contagious, and after a while, her ass even started to depress me.

Yesterday, I couldn't take it anymore. I was tired of being

bored, so after spending $500 at the spa for a French manicure, pedicure, bikini wax, and a two-hour Swedish massage, I was ready to go out, and I knew Osha's ass was coming with me, whether she liked it or not. When I asked her about it, she came up with a thousand and one reasons why she couldn't go, but I wouldn't take no for an answer. I snatched that dumb-ass Kindle out of her hand, dragged her ass out of bed, and damn near pushed her stinky ass into the shower. I told her she had an hour and a half to get dressed, and if I had to come back and get her, it wouldn't be pretty. She ended up cooperating, with a little time to spare. I guess she knew I wasn't playing with her ass.

We ended up at this club called Studio 54. The theme and show for the night was "Electric Dream," and the club was fucking bananas! There were acrobats flying all around, doing crazy tricks and shit, but the white people loved it, and so did I. Neon lights bounced all around, lighting the place up. There were chicks on pedestals, dancing in halter tops, short skirts, and glittery thigh-high boots. There were five dance floors, so even though the place was packed, we could always find room to dance. Big projectors screens were everywhere, and the DJ played quite a variety of music. We danced to songs I've never even heard of, but all in all, it was a blast.

"Oh my God! My head is killing me," Osha says, staggering into the living area, dressed in a robe. Her hair is wild, and she has one earring dangling from her ear.

"Good afternoon, sleepy-head," I say, sitting on the couch drinking a hazelnut iced coffee, watching *Law and Order: SVU*.

"Afternoon? I've never sleep this late. What the hell did I do last night?" she asks, rubbing her eyes.

"We went to a club, and you, my dear…well, you're a wild child," I joke as I take a sip from my straw.

"What? What did I do?"

"For starters, you were taking off your clothes and grinding on some dude."

"Girl, you're lying!"

"I swear it's true. You acted a fool last night, Osha."

The look on her face is one of shock.

"Ol' dude left a little while before you woke up. He was a cutie too."

"I don't remember anything like that, and I only had one drink. I wonder what the hell the bartender put in it. I can't remember anything, and my head's throbbing." Her face turns serious. "Wait…ol' dude just left? What are you talking about? What dude?"

"The one you brought back to the room last night."

She doesn't say anything.

"The same guy you were all hugged up with in the club."

She just looks at me, utterly confused.

"You don't remember?"

"No! What the hell? I don't remember any of that!" She paces back and forth across the floor. "How could you let me leave with a perfect stranger, Brandy?"

"You're a grown-ass woman. What was I supposed to do? Tell you no?"

"You could've said something…anything! You shouldn't have let it go down like that. You're supposed to be my friend," she says, tears welling up in the corner of her eyes.

"Look here, Osha, I *am* your friend, but I'm not your babysitter. You can't expect me to jump between you and some guy you were practically fucking on the dance floor and tell you that you can't bring him into your room. If that's the kind of friend you want, you got the wrong bitch," I tell her seriously. "If you wouldn't have passed out drunk that night, would you have wanted me to tell Chad to leave?"

I told her Chad and Chino left right after she passed out. There was no need for her to know we fucked, especially since it was so quick and boring.

"You wouldn't have had to, because I would've made him leave myself."

"Girl, please! The way you were feeling him, his ass woulda been laid up right in that big-ass bed with you."

"Hell no he wouldn't have been! Yeah, I was feeling the dude, but it wasn't that serious. It was just something to do while we were here. He offered to buy us dinner, and I accepted. That's all. I swear I wouldn't have fucked him. I might talk a big game, but I'm not gonna play Taz like that. It just ain't right."

"I guess," I say, not believing a damn word of it.

She walks back and forth across the carpet, shaking her head. "I can't believe I did some shit like that."

"Calm down, girl. Damn! It's Vegas. You know the motto," I say, attempting to humor her a bit.

"Girl, I don't give a fuck about the motto. This is my life we're talking about. What if we didn't use a condom? What if he gave me something or I end up pregnant?"

"What if?" I parrot, shrugging, knowing there isn't anything we can do about it now.

"That's fucked up for real, Brandy. You know I'm with Taz."

"No, *you* know you're with Taz. That's *your* relationship, and if you can't respect it, what the hell you think I'm supposed to do about it? Speaking of Taz, isn't he the same nigga who hasn't answered any of your phone calls since we've been here? You don't even know what the fuck or who the fuck he's doing right now, and you're sitting here about to pull your hair out over nothing."

"Nothing? Do you think this shit is nothing, Brandy? What the hell is wrong with you?" she asks, looking at me with a wild look in her eyes. "As far as Taz is concerned, you let me worry about him."

"Wait a minute. You're mad at me now? For what? You're the one who fucked dude, not me. Maybe you should be mad at yourself, because I ain't have shit to do with that." I turn to walk away, knowing I better go to my room before I have to beat this bitch's ass.

"You know what, Brandy? Fuck you!" she yells in my direction. "You act like you're so much better than everybody else, but you ain't shit. This shit is serious to me, and here you are making light of the situation like my life can't be fucked up on the back of it! Not everybody wants to fuck with other people's men! I like sleeping with the same man night after night. I'm happy being wifey, and I'm not about to let you or anybody else fuck that up!"

"Naw, fuck *you*, Osha! Who the fuck do you think you are, bitch? If I ain't shit, you really ain't shit." I walk back over toward her, till I'm standing only inches from her face.

The scary ho takes a step back.

"I'm not the one crying up in this bitch because I fucked a complete stranger. That's you, boo boo. You're right about me kicking it with other bitches' men, but you betta know I gets paid, baby, so I don't give a fuck about what you or anybody else has to say. Not once have you heard me complain about spending money. Why? Because I got it like that. I don't get an allowance because I don't play that shit! You're all content and floating on cloud nine just because you think you're somebody's wifey, but that ain't shit but a label." I hold my hand up in the air to stop her from butting in. "When there's a wedding band on that ring finger instead of a promise ring and you get that shit on paper, come holla at me. Till then, shut the fuck up with your preachy-ass bullshit. Now, I'm about to go back into my room before you get me out my hook-up and I fuck around and catch a case in Vegas. Enjoy the rest of your vacation," I tell her and head for the stairs.

When I get back into my room, I've gotta fight everything in me not to go back downstairs and blast that ho in the mouth. Even though I can't hear her, I know she's down there talking shit on the low, and that pisses me off. I pace my room, walking back and forth, back and forth, still amped outta my mind.

A migraine comes out of nowhere, and my head starts pounding. I try to massage my temples, but that don't do the trick like it usually does, and it feels like my shit is about to explode! I flip my purse over and empty the contents, but I don't see any aspirin or anything that might relieve this pain. I remember that my Imitrex is in my travel bag in the bathroom, so I race in there to get it. Fumbling like a crack-head with a new fix, I pull the top off and slide the tube into my nose and inhale the medicine slowly.

Feeling relieved and knowing my migraine is about to come to an end, I lie back on my bed and close my eyes. I start to calm down a bit, but I still can't believe Osha flipped on me the way she did. I also can't believe I stood there without knocking the shit out of her for thinking I'm lame or something. Osha doesn't have a damn clue how close she was to getting the brakes beat off her ass for talking slick. Next time she'll know, though, because if she ever comes at me sideways again, it's going down!

About an hour later, I'm completely calm, and my migraine is gone. Even though she pissed me off, I know I've got the upper hand right now, and she'll figure that out as soon as we get back home. *Little Miss Perfect my ass! Osha ain't shit but a ho on the low.* You should've seen the way she was grinding on dude's dick last night while they were sitting in the chair. If they hadn't been wearing clothes, anybody woulda thought they was fucking right then and there. My mouth dropped when he popped one of her titties out on the dance floor and started nursing like a baby in front of the whole damn club. She started kissing him all over the neck, rubbing her hands through his hair and shit, loving every minute of it. Everybody thought they should get a room, and in the end, they did: hers.

I can't wait till Taz finds out what kind of bitch he's wants to claim as his woman. He's going to drop her wack ass so fast she won't even know what hit her. I know, because I'm going to make sure of it.

CHAPTER 14

We've been back in Ohio for about a week, and I haven't heard a thing from Osha. That's cool, though, because I don't need the bitch anymore anyway. She already fulfilled her purpose, and now it's time to cancel her ass like Nino did that light-skinned chick in *New Jack City*. I laugh out loud when I think about her refusing to speak on the plane, like that made any difference to me. I ain't got shit to say to her anyway, so I just lay back and closed my eyes throughout the entire flight. When we landed, I hopped right in a cab without saying a word. I wasn't gonna give that ho the benefit of even *thinking* I needed her bum ass to take me home. I still can't believe she spouted off at the mouth like that, and she's lucky I didn't break her bony ass in half.

It's about 3 o'clock when I step out of Tresses, and it's taken about two hours for me to get all my shit hooked up. Irritated, I toss the hair that's starting to stick to the side of my face over my shoulder. I don't understand why it's so fucking hot out, and I'm starting to think I should've gotten something up and off my neck instead of this wrap, because it's making me sweat like hell.

I hit the remote on my key ring to deactivate my alarm. I'm in the process of stepping into my truck when I see a young girl enter the shop with a bunch of purses on her arm. She comes back out and grabs two huge black bags out of the trunk of her car, then walks back inside. I figure she's some kind of booster, and since I'm never one to pass up a chance to spend money, I rethink leaving and head back into the shop myself.

It's a frenzy inside, and bitches are everywhere. There is merchandise all over the tables in the waiting area, and from all the people scurrying around, chattering like squeaky mice, you'da thought they were giving out free cheese. Those thirsty hoes are on it. From where I'm standing, the shit looks official, but I can't be sure until cop a feel and really get a good look at them. I overhear that the purse girl's name is McKenzie. When somebody asks her the price on a black Marc Jacobs bag, she says it's $200. I'm not sure if it's genuine or a knock-off, but the real thing would easily go for a little more than $1,000. *If she's giving deals like this away, I'm about to be hooked! I really wish these bums would hurry the hell up and get outta my way, because I'm ready to see what else she has.* After ten minutes of tapping my feet, waiting impatiently for those raggedy hoes to finish rummaging, the area is finally clear.

· "What you need, ma?" she asks.

"I'm not sure. There's so much. What you got?"

Without answering, she pulls more things out of bags and starts holding them up for me to see. She looks really young and can't be older than eighteen. She's pretty, with blemish-free, light skin and a baby face. Her hair is dyed a bronze color and styled in kinky twist, pulled back in a ponytail with a few stray braids framing her face. She's the same height as me but a little thicker than I am. All I see when I look at McKenzie are those hips and that ass. She isn't built weird or anything, and it actually looks good on her. I'm just shocked because I've never seen a woman with so much ass.

While she's pulling more things out of her bag, I check her outfit out. It's cute and pricey, and it's clear she's a young woman of taste. A pair of white crocheted Ralph Lauren sandals are on her feet, tied up the all the way to her calf. The silk halter dress would look a lot better if she had some kind of cleavage, but since she's flat-chested as hell, I guess she works with what she's had. The fabric is tie-dyed and bright as hell but cute—so cute that I've gotta laugh, because I just ordered the same one online from Saks, and that bitch was $800! Either business is booming, or baby girl can steal her ass off!

"I got anything you need. What size do you wear?"

I give her my size, and she starts mixing and matching. In the end, I buy $5,000 worth of shit and only spend $1,500. McKenzie is a bad bitch when it comes to stealing, because she has anything and everything I could have ask for. Before we part, I store her number in my phone and promise that I'll call her tomorrow. She's going to be back at the mall, and I want to put my bid in. Fuck what you've heard. With prices like that, I've gotta be a loyal customer.

I put all my bargains in the trunk and drive off, then hop on the freeway to head home.

By the time I lug all those boxes upstairs into my apartment, I'm tired as hell. Sitting in the middle of my snow-white leather sectional, I twist off the top of my bottled water and take a long swig. By the time its back in an upright position, the damn thing is almost gone; I guess I was thirstier than I thought. I tilt it back one more time and place the empty bottle on the glass coffee table in front of me, then slide off my brown leather Jimmy Choo wedges and massage my aching feet.

"Ugh," I groan when a picture of Xavier pops into my head. The night he gave me a full body massage is a night I won't soon forget.

I make my way into my bedroom and place my shoes inside the closet before heading into my bathroom. Standing in front of the mirror, I use a wooden paddle brush to wrap my hair. It takes a little while because it's so soft, but I finally finish and secure it with a silk scarf. After I undress, I go back into my room and look in my dresser for something to wear. Snug in my baby-blue La Perla pajamas, I grab a pair of scissors from the nightstand and ready myself to get to work. Sitting on the edge of my bed, I prepare to cut open the many boxes I just brought up from my trunk. It takes me about an hour, but when I'm done, I'm quite pleased with the four stacks of clothes: shirts, pants, dresses, and underwear, all stacked neatly on one corner of my bed. In the opposite corner are purses, belts, and a few pairs of shoes. I smile, because I'm happy that all my shit is here and nobody was smart enough to steal it off Sade's porch.

When I got back from Vegas, I put Chad's American Express to work and ordered a bunch of stuff online. I had it delivered to Sade's house so nobody can trace it back to me. Since she's in jail, she's not gonna be home anytime soon, so I figure it's pretty fool-proof. Yesterday I received a notification to the email address I made up for the account, telling me everything would be delivered this morning. I dropped by before I went to the shop and was glad to see the delivery man had been there already. Since Sade lives in a decent neighborhood, nobody bothered the packages; had it been in the 'hood, my shit woulda been long gone. I didn't hesitate to back my truck up the driveway and loaded it all up.

It takes me forever to put everything away because I have to hang up the majority of it. My bedroom closet's been stuffed full since I moved in, so I have to lug everything into the fourth bedroom, which I've customized into a huge walk-in closet. That bitch looks like a boutique or some shit, and I got so much in there that it don't make no damn sense. It was already full as hell, but now it's overflowing because I went H.A.M on his card! I'm glad he uses American Express, because Visa woulda stopped my shop-till-I-drop ass long before I ever hit the $50,000 mark. I'm sure he doesn't have a clue, and by the time he finds out, there won't be shit he can do about it anyway. I always make sure to cover my tracks because I'm that bitch!

I blew a little more than five stacks in La Perla alone buying underwear, bras, and lingerie. I picked up thirty pairs of jeans: True Religion, 7 for All Mankind, Citizens of Humanity, Black Label, and Stella McCartney, about $20,000. I got this fly-ass $2,000 Burberry lambskin coat that was calling my name, a few Polo shirts, and quite a few blouses. I've got about ten new dresses, including the one McKenzie was wearing, two pairs of Sergio Rossi knee-high boots, a couple pairs of heels, and some black, thigh-high Christian Louboutin boots that fit perfectly when I tried them on. Of course shopping's only good for me when I pick up a couple fly-ass bags along the way, so I bought five of them, along with wallets to match.

After smashing the sweet and sour chicken and fried rice I had delivered from the Chinese spot, I undress and step into a hot bath. My body instantly relaxes, and I lie back, resting my head on the bath pillow.

Cachet

I close my eyes and start to think about Taz. I wonder what happened when he saw the tape I sent him a few days ago. I mailed it off the same day we got back, so I'm sure he's gotten it by now. I only hope Osha's thirsty ass didn't intercept it and toss it out before he had a chance to see it. Of course, it don't matter if she did, because I'll just send another copy. One way or another, he'll see that tape, if he hasn't seen it already.

You're probably wondering what tape I'm referring to. Since yo' nosy ass is all up in my business, I'll tell you. I'm sure you remember the argument that bitch Osha and I had at the MGM Grand. Well, earlier that night, at the bar, I slipped some Rohypnol into her drink. When I started to notice her getting drowsy, I grabbed this thirsty-looking dude who'd been staring at her the whole night and told him she was feeling him. He was all for it, especially when I told him she was looking for a hook-up that night. They danced for about thirty minutes and freaked out for a while before she started nodding. I told him it was time to go and helped him carry her up the stairs. Once we got inside the room, he asked me if she was all right, and I told him she always gets drunk off her ass like that. That was all he needed to hear.

He was kind of hesitant when I pulled out the video camera. I guess he thought I was going to do something crazy to him. I just explained to him that we do things like that all the time when we get wasted because we think it's funny to look at what we did the night before. He looked like he didn't believe me, but then Osha pulled his face to hers and kissed him roughly on the lips. After that, it was on. Before I started recording, I told him what to do, because I wasn't planning on speaking a word once the camera was rolling. To make it look good, I offered him the $1,000 Chad had given me, and he gladly accepted.

I watched as he damn near made love to her, just like I told him to, like it wasn't their first time having sex. I wanted Taz to think she'd been fucking around the whole time we were in Vegas. Even though she was out of it, it was too dark in the room for anybody to tell. I made sure to take a couple shots of her face, just so Taz knows it's her, but other than that, I only concentrated on their bodies. He flipped her over and hit it from the back, and she moaned like she was enjoying it. I recorded for about an hour and a half, and he followed all my instructions to the tee. I decided to wrap it up after he tittie-fucked those big jugs of hers and busted all over her chin. After I stopped rolling, I thanked him for his time, paid him his money, and kicked his ass out. That was shady as fuck, right?

Yeah, I think so too.

After finishing my bath, I pat my body dry before sliding my feet into my red Etro slippers and wrapping my body with the matching robe; I tie it at the waist. I saunter into the kitchen and grab a cold bottle of water and a bag of pretzels before heading back into my bedroom. I prop a few pillows up and climb under the covers, naked. I open the bag of pretzels and power up my fifty-five-inch LG plasma.

After about an hour of aimlessly watching TV, I decide to give Taz a call. I'm absolutely sure he's gotten the video by now. My question is: Why hasn't he called me yet? I pick up my cell phone and scroll down to his name and hit send. It rings three times before he answers.

"What's up?" he asks.

"Hey, what you doing?"

"Nothing."

"Okay, well, where are you?"

"The crib," he answers.

I can tell he's being short. "*The* crib or your crib?" I ask, getting irritated. I don't know why the fuck he's acting all funny toward me and shit. Any other time I call, he's running his damn mouth a mile a minute, trying to keep me on the phone.

"Mine."

There he goes with those short answers and shit. I can't take it anymore. "What the hell is wrong with you?"

"Shit."

"Do you got a problem with me or something? Because if so, you need to say that shit. You really starting to get on my nerves with these short-ass answers, Taz!" I yell into his ear.

"Naw, you good."

"All right. Fuck it, Taz. You just call me when you feel like talking, because this shit here is blowing me."

"Bet," is all I hear before my phone makes the noise that lets me know the call has been disconnected.

I pull the phone away from my ear and stare at is like it's an alien or some shit. It's on the home screen, so I know for sure his bitch ass hung up on me. I sit in shock for a second before placing my phone on the nightstand. *I can't believe that muthafucka had the nerve to hang up in my face! I don't know what the hell his problem is, but I'm the wrong bitch to take it out on. He acts like I'm bothering him or something, and I'm feeling some kinda way because he brushed me off quick as fuck! What the hell is his problem anyway?* I snatch my phone back up and start to call his ass back just to dog the fuck out of him, but I change my mind. I'm not about to give him the benefit of knowing he pissed me off, so I lay it back down.

After adjusting my pillows, I lie back and snuggle up under the cover and close my eyes. That's when it hits me: *What if he knows I'm the one who sent him the tape and he's pissed? Better yet, what if he knows I drugged Osha and they're plotting to do something to me?* All these questions are floating around in my head, and even though I'm paranoid, I'm sure neither of them is happing. *Maybe he's going through some shit and wants to be left alone. Yeah, that's what it is.* Even though that makes the most sense to me, it still doesn't give that bastard a reason to treat me this way. Without a doubt, I know he'll call me before I call his ass, and when he does, it's gon' be hell to pay! It only takes me a few minutes of lying down before I'm tired enough to fall asleep and when I do, I'm out like a light.

CHAPTER 15

2003…

Pitch laughs when he sees the wet spot appear in the middle of my legs.

"What ya scared for, bitch?" he asks.

I don't say anything because I'm too scared. I just look at Trixie, hoping she'll do something, because I know he plans to kill us both. Either that, or he's going to make us wish we were dead. The look on her face tells me just what I'm thinking: It's about to go down!

"Give me my fucking money, Brandy!" he roars so loudly I almost jump out of my skin.

I extend my hand toward him, but Trixie grabs my wrist, stopping me. She steps directly between the two of us.

"What the hell you think you doing, Trix?"

"I'm not going to let you hurt her, Pitch. She's just a kid. Please just let her go. Don't do this," she begs.

"Get the fuck out my way, Trixie. I'll deal with yo' lying ass in a minute."

She doesn't budge.

He hauls off and smacks her so hard that her head jerks

Cachet

back violently. She loses her balance and stumbles back, falling into the wall with a loud thud. *Recovering quickly, she runs back over to him with the fury of a crazed woman. She scratches and punches with everything in her, on him like a fly on a fresh pile of shit; I've never seen her so mad. The hits don't faze Pitch, and he shows it by laughing out loud. Pitch continues to block her hits left and right. Even though he's laughing, there ain't nothing funny. He's downright angry.*

"Run, Baby Doll! Get out of here!" she yells, but I stay stuck in the same place for a while, and my legs won't move. I hear, "Run, Baby Doll!" again, and that's when I take off down the stairs and out the door.

I make it to the middle of the circle driveway before I realize I can't leave her there with him. I know he'll kill her. I turn around and race back into the house, heading straight for the family room. I grab one of the chrome fireplace pokers out of the rack and run back up the stairs as fast as I can. He's kneeling over her, with his hands wrapped tightly around her neck. I stop to catch my breath for only a second, then run over toward them, holding the poker high above my head. Nothing but a grunt is heard when I bring my weapon down and across his back, and he still doesn't release his hold. When that doesn't faze him, I continue to strike him repeatedly with everything in me; I have to get him off of her.

After a dozen hits, he frees her from his grasp and falls to the ground himself. Trixie's head drops to the floor with a thud, *and she doesn't move. Pitch begins to stir and starts to slowly lift himself off his back and onto his knees. The fear in me kicks in, and I swing the poker again, this time hitting him right in the back of the head; he falls, knocked out cold.*

When I see that it's safe, I run over to Trixie and lift her head into my hands. Calling her name and shaking her doesn't work, so I make my way into the bathroom. I grab a cup and fill it with water and hurry back down the hall. I toss the cold water onto her face and jump back when she bolts upright and clutches her neck, choking.

"Oh my God! I'm so glad you're okay!" I throw my arms around her shoulders, careful not to stick her with the poker.

"Where's Pitch?" she asks, breaking my hug and frantically looking around. When her eyes land on his slumped-over body, she leaps up, grabs my hand, and drags me toward the stairs.

Before we make it to the first step, she drops my hand and tiptoes slowly over to where my father is lying. I watch her, confused but more scared, praying he doesn't wake up and catch her. My knuckles turn white around my death grip on the poker. I have plans to beat the hell out of him if he so much as moves a muscle.

Trixie reaches into his pants pocket and pulls out a set of keys. A small stack of money is retrieved from the other pocket, and she tucks it into her bra. Next, we make our way down the stairs. Outside, she hits the alarm on the keys, and the black Cadillac Deville responds.

"Do you still have the money I gave you?" she asks as we climb inside the luxury vehicle.

"Yeah, it's in my pocket. Where are we going?"

"We're going to a hotel for a few days, until I figure something out."

As we pull out of the driveway, I glance back at the house I've grown to love and hate; before long, it begins to disappear.

Cachet

***

It's been two months, and we've been staying at the Super 8 in Twinsburg. It's not really far from where Pitch lives, so I'm always on edge. Every time I hear the slightest noise in the hallway, I almost have a heart attack. Trixie says I'm paranoid and that he won't find us, but I know better.

I remember the first night we got here. Trixie dropped me off and came back close to an hour later. She told me she parked the car on a deserted street a few miles from where we were and caught a cab back. I cried that night and told her he was going to find us and that he'd kill me when he did. She held me close and guaranteed that he would have to kill her first. I didn't say anything, but I figured he would do that anyway.

The room is dark as I lie in bed, pretending to sleep. Trixie is sitting in the brown chair in the corner, just staring out the window. A glimmer of moonlight enters the tiny room, and I see a tear roll slowly down her beautiful face; she looks worried. She has the same thing on her mind as I do: How are we going to survive? When we first got here, we had a little over four grand, but that money is dwindling, and we almost have nothing left. We've spent at least $3,000 staying here, and the room is only $50 a night. Add in a few outfits, food, and personal items, and you can see what I mean. We only have $500 left, and that's only enough to pay for ten more days, not even including food. I'm scared to ask what we're going to do when that runs out, because I really don't want to know the answer.

HEARTLESS

* * *

A week later, I wake up to Trixie getting dressed. "Good morning, Baby Doll," she says in a chipper voice.

"Good morning." I sit up and rub the sleep from my eyes before I ask, "Where are you going today?"

"To the same place I've been going for the last week, out to get us some money."

For the past week, Trixie has been hitting the track, just to make sure we'll be okay. She didn't want to tell me at first, but I wouldn't let up, and she ended up spilling the beans. I told her I would help by getting a job, but she refused. Selling her body is all she knows how to do, and she says she's going to do that until she can't anymore. Even though it's a terrible thing to do, I've gotta respect her for it.

"You're leaving me again?"

"Yes, but not for long. I'll be back before it gets dark." She puts on her coat and pulls her hair out, letting it cascade down her back. She looks over at me and smiles when she sees me looking at her. "What are you looking at, Baby Doll?"

"You. You're so pretty," I tell her truthfully.

"Well thank you, but you're not too bad yourself."

I giggle.

"For real, Baby Doll. You are beautiful, and one day you'll see that."

"Thank you."

She turns to leave, but I don't want her to—not today. I've got a bad feeling about it. Even though everything has been cool for the past week, I'm still nervous.

"Don't go, Trixie. We can just stay here and watch movies and eat popcorn. I still have two bags left."

Cachet

"We'll do that when I come back. I promise." She walks over to me and kisses me on the forehead. "I love you, Baby Doll."

"I love you too," I reply to her back as she walks out the door.

Nightfall comes, and I still haven't heard a thing from Trixie. I sit there worrying, watching out the window, but I'm not worried about money; I'm worried about her. I figure time will go by quicker if I distract myself from worrying, so I decided to watch a bit of TV. A movie called Double Jeopardy, *with Ashley Judd and Tommy Lee Jones, is on. Normally, I wouldn't even give it a second glance, but since there's nothing else on, I decided to watch it. I must've fallen asleep, because by the time I woke up, it was daylight, and Trixie was still not back. I started crying. I knew there was something wrong, because otherwise, there was no way she would've left me alone all night. She promised me she'd be back before dark, and Trixie never breaks her promises.*

Where could she be? I searched around the room for clues as to where she may have gone, but I came up empty. Too afraid to go outside, I sit in the room and cry until I can't cry anymore.

* * *

Minutes turn to hours and hours to days, and there's still no sign of Trixie.

A knock on the door startles me. I'm not sure who it is, but figuring it might be someone who knows something about Trixie, I manage a weak, "Who is it?"

"Hotel management, ma'am."

I walk over and peer out of the peephole. When I see the

guy from the front desk, I open the door.

"Hey, I was just comin' by to remind you that you haven't paid for your week yet," he says.

He's a dark-skinned older black guy, and he wouldn't be bad-looking, except for the rotten teeth in his mouth. He looks to be in his mid forties, and I'm sure he works out, because his body was toned. He's sporting a baldy, but I can tell his hair was already thinning before he made the decision to cut it. I gag at the smell coming from his mouth; his breath smells like month-old horse shit.

"Are you sure?" I ask, taking a step back.

"Yes, ma'am. The woman who shares the room with you usually comes in and pays for the week on Sundays by 9 a.m., but it's Monday, almost 4:00. I was supposed to come up yesterday, but I wanted to give her the benefit of the doubt, thinking maybe she forgot. If ya don't come down and pay within the next hour, I'm afraid I'm gonna have to ask you to leave."

"Okay. I'll be down in a minute," I say and close the door.

I scamper around the room once again, looking for something, for anything. I know I have to give the man some money, or he's going to put me out, along with mine and Trixie's stuff. Searching high and low, I open everything I can find, on the hunt for money, but I come up with nothing. I pray that Trixie will show up soon, because I don't know what I'm going to do if she doesn't.

An hour later, another knock comes at the door. My eyes are red from crying, and my head is pounding, because I know it's the hotel manager coming to give me the boot.

"I thought you were coming down," he asks as soon as I open the door.

"I was, but my mother hasn't gotten back yet. She has all the money with her," I lie.

"I understand that, but the hotel needs to be paid right now." The look on his face tells me he doesn't believe me, probably because he hasn't seen Trixie in almost a week.

"Can you give me a few more hours?"

"I'm sorry, young lady, but you either gotta pay for the day right now or go."

"What am I supposed to do?" I ask, like he actually has the answer to my question.

"I'm not sure, but you have to vacate this room if you can't pay. Come on. I'll help you pack up your belongings." He pushes his way past me to enter the room.

While he stands in the middle of the room looking around, I look down at the floor because I'm too embarrassed to look him in the eye. I can't help but notice the new pair of Jordans on his feet, black with white soles decorated with a red flame shape. His red shirt has "Harold Scott" written in bold white letters and is tucked neatly into a pair of dark blue Levi's. Just by looking at him, I can tell he's one of those old guys who's trying to hold on to his youth by dressing like the younger generation

"Please don't make me leave, mister. I don't have anywhere to go." I begin to cry. When his face softens , I go in for the kill. I hope if I tell him my story, maybe he'll let me stay. "I can't go back ho-home because my father is going to…to… to force me back into prostitution. Me and Trixie stole money from h-him and now he wants to ki-ki-kill us. I-I-I ran away fr-from him because he raped me and wa-was trying to make me have sex for mo-mo-money. If you put me out, I-I don't know what will happen to me!" Tears are running rapidly down my face, and I can't bare to say another word because I'm crying so hard. Snot is coming out of my nose and sliding down my bottom lip, but I don't care. I need him to understand that I can't leave this hotel room, because I'll die on those streets.

He walks over to me and takes me into his arms. The smell of his cologne masks the funk coming from his mouth. "It's okay. It's gonna be okay." He pats my back gently. "We'll work out something."

"For real?" I look up with hopeful eyes.

"You can stay tonight, and we will work out something for tomorrow."

I'm so happy that I can't contain myself. After he leaves, I lie back on the bed with a smile on my face. He told me we'll work something out, and I don't care if it's a cleaning job or working at the front desk. Whatever it is, I'll do it.

Even though I'm happy to be staying, I still worry and wonder about Trixie. I pray Pitch hasn't gotten to her, because if he has, I know I'll never see her again.

* * *

It's 9 o'clock a.m. when my sleep is broken by a knock on the door. When I see the hotel manager through the peephole, I open the door, and my nostrils are immediately assaulted by his bad breath. I wonder, doesn't this guy believe brushing his teeth or at least chewing gum?

"Hello, mister." I pause.

"Harold. Just call me Harold," he tells me with a rotten-toothed smile.

"Hello, Harold. How can I help you?"

"I figured out how you're going to pay your way around here."

Cachet

My stomach drops from the way he says it; he sounds the same way Pitch did when he broke the news to me that he was gonna send me out on the track.

"Um, okay. How is that?" I'm scared of the answer.

"You're going to work for me."

"What do I have to do?"

"Let me step in, and I'll tell you."

"Why do you have to step in? Why can't you just tell me from out there?" I ask, tired of beating around the bush. Using my hip, I block the door so he can't push his way in like he did yesterday.

"Because I don't want the other guests to hear about our deal."

"Just tell me."

"Let me in, or the deal is off," he booms, and I know he's serious.

Even though I don't want to, I allow him to enter.

"Okay. What is it?" I ask with attitude when he sits on my bed. My hands are on my hips as I stare at him, pissed and awaiting his answer.

"Well I was thinking, since you don't have anywhere else to go, you'd probably do almost anything to stay here."

My stomach drops again.

"So I came up with the perfect deal. You service me a few times a week, and I'll let you stay here for as long as you want. I'll even include meals."

Oh my God! Not again! "Service you how?"

"You know what I mean, but since you're pretending you don't, let me break it down for you. Have sex with me—you know, suck my dick and whatever else I want." He licks his lips. "You do that, and I'll pay your way around here." He

stands up and walks over toward me.

I back up slowly into the corner. "And what if I say no?" I ask, because this shit is not about to happen.

"Then I'll have to call the police and tell them you haven't paid for your room in two days and you won't leave. I'm sure they'll just take you back to your father's house, and they'll want to know why a minor is staying at a hotel by herself anyway. From what you told me yesterday, I'm sure Daddy will be more than happy to see you." He gives me that rotten-ass smile again. "Think about it, I'll be back in an hour." He walks out the door, not even bothering to close it behind him.

After I close and lock the door, I drop to the floor and cry.

How dare he use what I've told him against me? Why are people so cruel? Why is it that everywhere I turn, someone always wants something from me? This is just more proof that I can't trust anyone. Yesterday, he was Mr. Nice Guy and had me thinking he was going to save me. Now, I see that he's just like the rest. All he wants is what I can give him. This must be the way of life: You've gotta do something in order to get something in return. That has to be it, because that's all I've seen.

What am I going to do? Going back to Pitch is not an option because I know he'll just kill me for what I've done. I can't just leave, because I have nowhere else to go. I don't know a soul, and the only person who's ever had my back is gone; I'm not even sure she's still alive. I fight with myself for a few minutes about what to do, and then I finally come up with an answer.

A while later, the door opens, and in walks Harold with a key in his hand; he didn't even bother to knock this time. I guess he figures there's nothing I can do about it, so he can do what he wants. "So...what's it gonna be?" he asks, running his hands through my hair like he owns me or something.

I don't say anything at first because vomit moves up in my throat, making it hard to swallow. I can tell by the irritated look on his face that the suspense is killing him, so I finally answer with words that kill me to the core. "I guess I don't have a choice, I'm going to stay."

CHAPTER 16

A loud noise awakens me from yet another nightmare. I look up and realize it's only a commercial; I fell asleep with the TV on last night. These dreams are going to have to stop, because if they don't, I may fuck around and lose my goddamn mind! Every time I fall asleep, it's as if I'm being forced to relive the life I so desperately want to forget. I know I can't change the past, but I damn sure want to move on from it. Hell, I wanna at least live somewhat of a normal life. I'm tired of waking up with tears all over my face. That all happened a long time ago, and I just want it to leave me the hell alone so I can live normal. Is that too much to ask for? The part that really scares me is the fact that there's so much more to these stories. *What's going to happen when I dream of those?* I have to wonder. "Ugh!" I scream in frustration.

The clock reads 12:00, noon, and I still can't believe I almost overslept. I have a doctor appointment at 1:15, so I know my ass better get to moving. I really need to get these migraines checked out, because it could be something much worse than I think.

After brushing my teeth and washing my face, I walk over

to my closet and try to find something to wear. It takes me an hour to shower, do my hair, and get dressed, so it's around 1:05 by the time I finally leave my house. I push the elevator button repeatedly, hoping like hell I make it to the clinic by 1:30. If not, I know whoever is at the front desk will make me reschedule, and I don't want that. Like I said, I really need to see the doc, so I know I've gotta get my sleepy ass in gear.

It's 1:25 when I fly through the parking lot of the Neighborhood Family Practice building on Ridge Road. My ass only has five minutes to spare at the most. When I see a parking space ahead of me, I turn my wheel and prepare to whip into it.

I'm forced to slam on my brakes when a little Puerto Rican boy runs out and stops right in front of my truck. He looks to be about two or three, because he's so small. He turns to take off running but loses his footing, trips, and falls flat on his face, right by my front tire.

I throw my truck in park and jump out when I hear him scream; I need to make sure he's all right. "Are you okay?" I ask.

He doesn't say anything because he's still screaming and crying. Looking around, I don't see anyone in sight, so I bend down and pick him up. His cheek is bleeding slightly, and his hands are really red. I place the kid on the driver seat of my truck, then open the middle console and remove a Kleenex. Using the open bottle of water in my cup holder, I wet it and place it gently on his bruised skin. "Ouch!" he says, but he stops complaining once the coolness of the water stops the sting. A smile covers his face, and for the first time, I really take a good look at him. He's so damn cute! He has chubby cheeks and bright green eyes attached to long, thick eyelashes, so bushy they look fake. Tight black curls are all over his head, and if I didn't know any better, I'd swear up and down that he's a girl.

"Does that feel better?" I ask, fixing the collar of his yellow Ralph Lauren shirt.

"Yes," the boy replies, still smiling.

"Do you want a piece of gum?" When he nods, I reach into my purse and dig around.

After peeling back the silver foil, he puts the piece of Winterfresh in his little mouth and begins to chew it.

"*Qué demonios estás hacienda con mi bebé?*" I hear over my shoulder.

I turn around and come face to face with a short, evil-looking Puerto Rican woman. If not for the scowl on her face, she'd look like the older version of him. Her long hair is pulled back into a curly ponytail that rests over her left shoulder. She's dressed in a black Juicy Couture track suit and a pair of Prada sneakers.

I roll my eyes, because I know this li'l bitch is going to take me there. "Excuse me?" I ask, looking down at her; I don't understand Spanish.

"You heard me. What the hell are you doing with my baby?" she repeats, in English this time. It kind of makes me wonder why the fuck she started talking to my black ass in Spanish in the first place.

"Your *baby* ran out in front of my truck, tripped, and hit his face on the concrete."

"Fine, but that's not what I asked. What the hell are *you* doing with him?"

I sigh, trying to remain calm. "Well, how about I ask *you* a question?" I take a step toward her but keep my eye on him; I don't want him to fall out of the truck. "Where the hell were you while he was running around in the fuckin' street?"

Her face shows shock, but she doesn't back down and only takes a step closer. "That's none of your concern, but if you must know, I was minding my damn business. That's where I was." She laughs. "I didn't ask you to touch my fucking son, so keep your hands to yourself, *la puta*." She moves around me and holds her hand out for him to grab it. As soon as his hand touches hers, she snatches him out of the seat, almost knocking his poor little arm out of the socket in the process.

"What the fuck is wrong with yo' dumb ass? You could've hurt him!" I yell as she walks away.

She doesn't pay me any attention. Instead, she continues to drag him behind her like a ragdoll as he struggles to keep up.

I can hear her talking shit the entire way, even though I can't understand her. I would walk over to her and get in her face, but I'm late enough. I swear, if I had ten more minutes, I would get in her ass! I don't even think it would matter, because this ho gon' be a terrible mother no matter what. Some people just aren't fit to have children, and this bitch is one of them; I still want to kick her ass though.

I climb back into the driver seat and pull the rest of the way into the parking space before turning off the engine. I lock my doors and get out, then put a little bit of pep in my step, trying to make it into the building before I'm forced to reschedule. By the time I get in the building and through the line, it's 1:40.

The extremely obese chick at the front counter looks behind her at the time and says, "You're twenty-five minutes late."

"I know, but it wasn't my fault. See, there was this kid, and—" I try to explain.

"I'm sorry, sweetie, but I'm gonna have to reschedule you because you're more than fifteen minutes late."

"Listen, I was here on time, but this little boy ran in front of my truck," I ramble. When I see it's not working, I try another tactic. "I really need this appoint—"

"Sorry, but those are the rules." She cuts me off without even giving me eye contact. She then hands me a printout with my new appointment date and time, without even asking me if the time slot she gave me is okay. Before I get a chance to protest, she calls the next person, dismissing the shit out of me.

I'm so pissed that I have to close my eyes and breathe, because this bitch is really taking me there. I swear, I hate ugly, fat bitches! She's just mad because she's all fucked up and can't look this good. It ain't my fault I was blessed with beauty, and taking her ugliness out on me is a bunch of bullshit! I know I was more than fifteen minutes late, but hell, it really wasn't my fault. If I hadn't had to tend to that little boy in the parking lot, I would've made it inside on time. "What the fuck am I going to do now?" I whisper to myself.

I take a seat in a nearby chair and place my elbows on my lap, then use both hands to cover my face. I slowly begin to massage my temples, trying to stop the headache that I feel coming on. I'm so mad that my body begins to rock back and forth like I'm some nutcase in a straitjacket. I attempt to calm myself down, but it does no good, because that Puerto Rican ho's face keeps popping up in my head. I'm so pissed! Not only did she make me late for my appointment, but she had the audacity to disrespect me in the process. I knew I should've beat her ass, especially since I ultimately had to reschedule anyway.

Finally, I stand up and make my way to the door, because it makes no sense to sit here if I'm not going to be seen. On my way out, I catch a glimpse of the cute little boy, sitting in the waiting area and reading a book. I scan the place a bit more

Cachet

and see his bitch mother a seat over, still wearing that same nasty scowl on her face. Either the bitch is always angry, or that look on her face is permanent. Either way, it's fucked up.

I turn to walk away, but my body won't let me; I have to go check this bitch! I quickly make my way over to her, scaring the shit out of her in the process. "What was that fly shit you was popping outside?" I ask.

"What?" She smirks.

"You heard me, bitch. It's your dumb-ass fault that I have to reschedule my appointment. Fucking around with you and your son…I should knock yo' ass out!" I can see a small amount of fear in her eyes. She's not completely scared, but I've got her shook enough.

"I wish you would, bitch," she counters, playing hard.

By now, everyone in the clinic is looking our way. They all want to see what's going to happen next. I don't give a damn though, because don't none of these muthafuckas know me. Taking a few steps toward her, I dare her to stand up, but of course she doesn't. She only sits and continues to look at me with that smirk on her face. That pisses me off, so I take a swing at her, but I don't connect because I'm hoisted off my feet by a pair of strong arms. I struggle to try to get away, but the hold is too tight. *Who the fuck has me?*

"Calm down!" I hear in a strong male voice.

"Fuck that *puta, papi*. Let her go!"

"Trust me, you don't want that," I warn from the air.

"Calm your ass down, Marissa!" the same voice says.

The bitch instantly shuts up.

"Let me go!" I yell.

"I will, but you're gonna have to calm down first."

"I don't gotta do shit but stay black and die!" I say smartly.

He laughs. "Well, I'm not letting you go till you settle down."

A couple seconds pass, and I don't say a word.

"See? That's better."

He places me down, and as soon as my feet touch the ground, I spin around, prepared to cuss his ass the fuck out. I stop before a word even leaves my lips because this man is gorgeous. He stands a few inches taller than me and has the body of a god! From the looks of his broad, strong shoulders, it seems he must work out daily in the gym. My lips curl into a smile, and I stare at this beautiful man in awe. He puts me in the mind of actor Adam Rodriguez, the guy who played Sandino in Tyler Perry's, *I Can Do Bad All by Myself.* He has the same crooked smile, bushy eyebrows, and blemish-free skin.

"What the hell you staring at, *puta?*" ol' girl speaks, breaking our intense stare down; I forgot all about her ass.

"What did you just say?" he asks.

She doesn't reply.

"Because last time I checked, I told you to calm your ass down!" he scolds. She scrunches her face up in disgust but says nothing. "Can I talk to you outside for a minute?" he asks me, and I nod.

"*Papi*, you got me fucked up! What you gotta go outside for?"

"Mari—" He tries to talk, but she cuts him off.

"*Por qué siempre ir esto a mí? Tu vas a hablar con esta puta delante de mí? Te juro que te odio!!*" she yells in her spoken language.

"Shut your fuckin' mouth, Marissa! I'll handle this," he says as we walk toward the door.

Cachet

Before we walk completely out, I turn to face her and smirk.

Once we're outside, I walk down just far enough so she can see us clearly through the window. I don't know who this guy is to her, but she's overprotective as hell, and I'm going to use that to piss her off even more. Why? Simple. Just because I don't like the ho. I place my back against the window and stare at him, waiting for him to start talking.

He utters no words and just stares at me intently, licking his lips. He's dressed in a black and red Aero sweatshirt, a pair of jeans, and butter Timberlands—plain but no less sexy.

"What's up?" I ask, breaking the silence.

"What happened back there?"

"What you mean?"

"Why are y'all angry and ready to fight?"

I think about not telling him, but I finally figure, what the hell? I go on to explain to him what's transpired since I pulled up. I tell him about the little kid being in the street by himself and that he fell down in front of my tire, after almost getting run over. I also mention that he was left unattended for quite a while before she finally came looking for him. "It had to have been a few minutes," I say. "If I were a kidnapper, he'd be long gone." Then I complain about her having the nerve to flip out on me, like I was the one who did something wrong. Lastly, I explain to him that the appointment I need so bad was canceled because of it, and that's another reason why I'm so upset with her.

Come to find out, the chick is this dude's baby-mama, so the little boy is his son. He tells me he just got here and walked in seconds before I ran up on her, so he didn't see what went on in the parking lot. He's pissed to find out how careless she's been with his child, and he promises to take care of it as soon as he goes back inside. I laugh to myself when he says it, because I believe without a doubt that he's going to beat her ass, and I ain't mad at him at all for that.

"How can I get to know you better?" he inquires.

"Start by asking for my number," I flirt.

"How about we lock in each other's?"

"Sounds good to me."

We each pull out our phones and pass them to the other. I push my number into his phone as Chocolate Goddess, then pass it back. He laughs when he sees that, then tells me it's true. When I check out my phone, I see that his name is Angel.

Minutes pass, and we stay outside and talk and laugh about random things. Out the corner of my eye, I see ol' girl staring hard as fuck, trying to see what we're talking about, so I give her what she's looking for. Cutting our conversation short, I tell him I have to go and that I'll call him later. After he tells me he understands, we prepare to part ways.

I start to walk away, then turn around and face him once more. "Can I have a hug before I go?" I ask.

"You can have whatever you like."

"Be careful what you promise. I just might take you up on it," I say, taking a few steps into his personal space.

"That's cool. I want you to."

We are now face to face, and I can smell the spearmint on his breath. "I like you."

"I like you too." He pulls me closer, placing his arms tightly around my waist. I like it, but I'm shocked; I mean, his baby-mama is just a few feet away. From where I'm standing, I can see she's watching his every move. He apparently doesn't care, and I damn sure don't, so we good. "Don't worry about her?" he says, as if reading my mind.

"What?"

"Marissa. Don't worry about her. She knows her place. She's my baby's mother and nothing more."

"She's not your woman?" I ask, taking a step back and placing my hands on my hips.

"No, nothing like that."

"You mean to tell me you don't have sex with her at all anymore?"

"I didn't say that. What I said is that she knows her place, and she's not my woman." He licks his lips. "She has my son, and I provide for the both of them. He doesn't want for anything, and neither does she, but I do what I want."

"I don't want no drama," I lie. My ass is all about drama. Hell, drama should be my middle name.

"You won't get any from me."

He smiles. "Well, in that case, I'll talk to you later."

I walk over to him once again and kiss him softly on the cheek before strutting away.

* * *

Later, I'm back at home, sitting on the couch and watching a rerun of *Maury*. Some fat, ugly-ass girl keeps running up to pictures on the monitor, trying to point out the fact that her son has the exact same nose as the presumed daddy. Maury asks her how sure is she that he's the father, and she replies, "I'm 1,000 percent sure," just like all the other 'hood rats who appear on the show daily. After a while, the guy comes out, calling the chick all kinds of bitches and hoes, telling the world how much of a slut she is and how he fucked her in the park on the first night. They argue so much that Maury doesn't wait until the commercial break to read the results. "In the case of Daniel Moore, Chris, you are NOT the father." The crowd begins to boo, and the guy jumps up and does the stanky leg. Of course the girl runs off the stage crying, like always, falling on the floor and hollering and all that shit. This damn show is so predictable, but I love it anyway.

My phone vibrates, alerting me I have a text message. I scroll down to see what it says:

Angel: *I been thinking about u all day.*

Me: *Is that right? What have u been thinking?*

Angel: *How good ur lips would feel against mines.*

Me: *Well, if ur a good boy, u won't have 2 wait 4 long. ;-)*

Angel: *Can I see u 2night?*

Me: *Time/place?*

Angel: *Sans Souci, downtown @ 9pm.*

Me: *Got it. CU then.*

I have a little over three hours to get dressed, and I'm going to put all that time to use. I plan on having fun tonight, and Angel is just the guy to make it happen. I don't know how much money he has, but I can tell he's working with something. Tonight I'm going to get to know him a bit more and see how valuable he is to me. If he's got a lot, I'll put him on the same list as Taz. If not, at least I'll get some dick.

* * *

It's been a little over a week since I've been talking to Angel, and I have his ass right where I want him. The first night, I went over to his house after dinner. I was expecting to get fucked all kind of ways, but truthfully, it was the worst sex I've ever had. He enjoyed it though, because I had him climbing the walls like a little bitch. He kept calling my name, telling me he was in love right after we were done. Usually, I'd dog the fuck out of a nigga like that and ignore his calls for being corny, but after what he told me at dinner, I decided to give him a chance: "I sell kush by the pound to almost everyone in the city of Cleveland," he said. Basically, in not so many words, he let me know he's that nigga. I still wasn't sure, and I don't fall for no bullshit, so I decided to find out for myself.

The day of truth came sooner than I thought. It was a Friday night, and we were sitting at his house watching *Weeds* on Showtime when his cell phone rang. He answered it, then told me he had to make a run. I made up a lie about having a headache, because I didn't want to go. What I really wanted to do was go through all his shit, and that was impossible while he was there. He disappeared for a minute, then returned with a book bag over his shoulder and told me he'd be back soon.

As soon as the door closed, I was up and all over the place. I swear I looked everywhere, but I didn't come up with nothing. Just when I decided to give up, I walked down the stairs and saw that the basement had a padlock on it. I don't know about you, but normal mu'fuckas don't put padlocks on just anything, unless it's important. I didn't know what was down there, but I was for damn sure going to find out. Ten minutes passed while I looked for a key, and I finally got tired and retreated back to the couch.

I gave up my search at just the right time, because minutes later, he walked back in the house. I watched him as he set the keys on the table and walked toward me. He smiled, grabbed my hand, and led me into the bedroom. I followed, and after I fucked him unconscious, I crept out of the room and made my way to his keys. Once I had an idea of which key it was,

I headed down the stairs, stuck it in the lock, and prayed it would work. To say I was overjoyed when I heard that *click* is an understatement. I opened the door, and when I finally found the light switch, I almost pissed on myself.

The wall on one side of the basement was lined with pounds of weed, so many pounds wrapped in Saran Wrap that it didn't make no damn sense! I assumed it was kush, because that was all he said he sold, but I wasn't really sure. I tried to come up with a ballpark figure on how much there was, but I couldn't because there were so many. It's safe to say he's that nigga in the weed game.

When I took my focus off that corner of the room and focused on the opposite side, I almost screamed. There were stacks upon stacks of money, wrapped in plastic, just like the weed. I walked over to the money slowly and picked up one of the packages. My first thought was to rob his ass blind, but I quickly realized there was no way in hell I was going to do that with him right upstairs.

It was then that the wheels in my head began to turn, and I knew I'd have to think of a fool-proof plan.

CHAPTER 17

A few minutes ago, I used the Spoof app on my phone to call Angel. During the call, I disguised my voice as a female customer who wants to buy a few pounds of kush tonight. He was hesitant at first, but as soon as I began to flirt with him, he agreed. I don't know how many times I've gotta say this, but dudes really need to learn to separate business from pussy. Fucking with pussy will get you got every time! I'm sure most of the niggas who used to be in the game fell off or got arrested or killed over one of three things: a hating-ass nigga, greed, or a bitch. It never fails. Niggas will do almost anything for a good piece of pussy, and I know Angel's no different, so I'm going to use that to my advantage.

I plan to be at his house before he leaves to meet the female that I pretended to be. Once he leaves, I'll take as much money as I can get my hands on. I'm sure he's going to be pissed once he finds out, but what the fuck is he really going to do? He doesn't know where I live or where I hang out. Hell, he doesn't even know my real name. From what I've told him, I live in Akron, I don't do clubs, and my name is Osha. I know it's fucked up, but I'm sure they'll never cross paths. Even if they do, he'll see that skinny ho and more than likely leave her alone. If not, oh well! Why would I trip about that? After I'm done with him, he won't be able to concentrate on retaliation because he'll be too busy trying to keep his ass out of jail.

I pick up my phone and call Angel to see what he's doing, because I really need to get over there. It's three hours before the meet time, and I want to be there way before then, so it won't look suspicious.

"*Hola, mami,*" he answers.

"What are you doing, *papi*?" I sing the name he prefers me to use when I talk to him.

"Sitting here smoking and watching *Scarface*. What you getting yourself into?"

"Hopefully your bed," I tease.

"Is that right? Well, how about you come over around 10:00, because I'm going to be heading out in a few," he says.

I can't go for that, because I need to get inside that house right now. "Aw. You don't wanna see me, *papi*?"

"Of course I do, *mi amore*. Why would you think I don't?"

"Because you've never told me to wait before, and I really want to see you," I whine.

"Stop that. You know I hate to see you disappointed. Okay. I'll see you in a few."

"Okay."

We disconnect the call, and I smile. *That was easier than I thought.*

I make it to his house at record speed because I don't want him to fuck around and leave. When I knock on the door, he swings it open, and I jump into his arms, wrapping my legs around his waist. *I have to play the shit out of this and make this nigga think I really missed him.*

HEARTLESS

With me still in his arms, he backs into the house and closes the door. He places my body up against the closed door, and we begin to kiss roughly, snatching off our clothes in the process. I slowly grind against his manhood, letting him know I want to fuck, and he responds like most men do: hard as a rock.

"Hold on, *mami*. Let me handle some business first. Messing with you will have me late to my meeting, and I'm going to get what I need so I can be ready."

I peep him grabbing his keys and making his way down the stairs. I'm sure he's going to get the weed he needs now so he won't have to do it later, and this works out better for me. Now all I have to do is figure out a way to get that damn key off of his ring before he leaves so I can get my shit!

I walk over to the couch and take a seat to wait for him. *Scarface* is playing in front of me, but I don't even pay it any mind. It's actually one of my favorite movies, but I have too many thoughts running through my mind to enjoy it.

I set up the meeting clear across town, so I know it's going to take him at least thirty minutes to get there. Once he does, he'll try to reach the customer by calling the number back, only to find that no one will answer. I know this because the number I used is a number to the small restaurant around the corner from my house. It's closed right now and doesn't have an answering machine, which is perfect. I can't have someone random person answering the phone and messing everything up. He'll call several times, I'm sure, because he won't want to leave without meeting her and getting his money, and I'm sure that will take at least twenty minutes. If I add thirty minutes for him to travel back, that gives me about an hour—an hour and a half, tops.

I know he might not be gone that long, so I'm planning for that also. I have to get as much money as I can into my truck, and I have an hour to do it. I brought some of my luggage and a few duffle bags, as that will make it easier for me to carry the cash. My pussy is dripping wet at the thought of all that money going into my bank account. I'm already good, but once I add this money, I'll be set. I won't even have to worry about Taz's ass anymore. He can keep his funky-ass attitude and chase after all those other hoes if he wants, because he'll be of no use to me once I rob Angel blind. If he calls me, I won't even answer. Truth be told, Osha can have his ass, as there'll be no use in me trying to sabotage their allegedly happy relationship that already went to shit a long time ago, starting with me fucking her man right under her nose.

A noise causes me to look toward the stairs, and when I do I see Angel coming back up the stairs. He walks past me with the same book bag in his hand that he had the other day, then disappears out the front door, only to return moments later. "Okay, where were we?" he asks, taking a seat beside me.

We lock lips again, before I push him back and straddle him.

"You are so fucking sexy."

"Only for you, *papi*."

Sitting on his lap, I grind slowly on his hard penis, moaning like crazy. My nails rake softly against his skin, and I lift his shirt up and over his head. Using my tongue, I trace small circles all over his chest, stopping to suck his nipple into my mouth. He moans as I flick my tongue back and forth across his, grinding harder. This only makes him more excited, and he begs me to let him fuck me. I don't say a word as I climb slowly off his lap. Keeping eye contact, I drop down to my knees in front of him. Unbuckling his belt is my first task, and I get it done in seconds. In no time, his pants and boxers are down around his ankles. His dick pulsates as I jerk it up and down with my hand, rubbing away the pre-cum with my thumb.

I drop my head into his lap and swallow his tool whole. You can take that literally, because his dick is so small it ain't no problem at all—like those damn Vienna sausages my mother used to make me eat. For the life of me, I can't understand how a man who's so damn fine can pack such a small pecker. I guess the world will never know.

"Ah! Suck *esta polla, mami,*" he says in half-Spanish, but even though I don't know what the fuck he's saying, I can tell he's loving it.

I continue to bob my head up and down in his lap while he shakes and shudders, trying to compose himself. When I feel as if he's about to cum, I take it up a notch and start to really tighten my jaw muscles. I wanna suck the life out of this muthafucka like a goddamn vampire so he'll be spent and won't know what's going on. The vein in his dick begins to throb and jerk, letting me know he's about to erupt at any minute. When he yells that he's cumming, I don't stop. Instead, I welcome it all into the back of my throat and swallow every drop. After I have him screaming and yelling for almost a full minute, I finally let up and stop the torture. He drops his head onto the back of the couch, and nothing can be heard but the sound of him breathing rapidly.

"Damn, *mi amore.* You sure know how to make a guy feel special." He smiles, showing off a perfect set of teeth.

"I think it's time for you to return the favor."

Without any words, he lifts me up from the floor and lays

me back on the couch. He carefully removes my Alexander Wang ankle boots and drops them on the floor beside him. Next he unbuttons my jeans, slides them down my legs, and tosses them clear across the room. As I lie here in a sweater and panties, I pray the man at least knows how to eat pussy, because I could go for a good nut right now. My body shivers in anticipation when he pulls my La Perla thong to the side and blows cool air onto my kitty. I feel his tongue begin to French kiss my pussy lips, and I close my eyes and bite down on my bottom lip. Rocking my hips back and forth, I hump his face and bring myself into my first orgasm.

Thirty minutes later, he's spent, exhausted, and pleasured on the couch. My head rests on his chest as it heaves up and down under me. As amazing as it is to say, I'm actually pleased with our sex. Angel can eat the hell out of some pussy. He had me screaming his name and clawing at the couch. Fucking him is usually wack as hell, because he has a dick the size of a toddler's, but I'm so turned on with the money that even that little muthafucka made me cum. I guess giving him one for the road was a good idea, and it will give him something to remember me by, as if stealing all of his money isn't a good enough memory.

"What time do you have to leave, baby?" I ask, looking at the cable box and already knowing he's got less than an hour to get to the meeting place.

"Shit! I need to get out of here in a few. You wanna ride with me?"

"Naw. I'm going to try to catch a nap, because when you come back, I'll be ready for round two," I lie. Little does he know, my ass will be long gone.

"I like the sound of that." He gives me a soft tap on the butt, letting me know he wants to get up, and I lift my body just enough for him to climb off the couch.

I watch him as he walks past me and into the bathroom. As soon as he's out of sight and out of earshot, I jump up and run over to his keys. Still naked from the waist down, I move as fast as I can trying to locate the key to the basement. When I find the one I'm looking for, I twist it around the key ring and remove it. When I hear the sound of the toilet flushing, I hurry and stick the key in my bra, then rush back over to the couch. It would be fucked up if I got caught right now. Not only would it mess up my plans, but I'm sure it would get my ass beat, and while his dick ain't nothing to write home about, the rest of his physique looks like he could do some damage. I climb back onto the couch and lie back, careful not to make too much noise in the process. For effect, I close my eyes and act like I'm sleeping. I don't open my eyes until I hear his zipper slide up.

"How long are you gonna be gone, *papi*?" I ask in a fake-ass sleepy voice.

"I'm not sure. Maybe an hour and a half. You want me to bring you anything?"

"Well, besides your fine-ass self, I'd love a chicken sandwich. You think you could stop at Burger King?"

"Sure."

"Okay. I like it with cheese…and I'd like a Sprite too." I place my order, knowing damn well it ain't gonna matter if I want fries with that, 'cause I ain't gonna be here when he returns with it.

"Got it," he says, then grabs his keys and walks out the door.

As soon as I hear his car start outside, I jump and begin

putting on my clothes. I move so fast that I think I put my panties on backward, but I don't care; I'll just fix them muthafuckas when I get home. I don't have a lot of time, and I want as much money as I can get. After grabbing my truck keys, I walk over to the door, open it, and peek out. I have to make sure the coast is clear, because I ain't trying to have his ass walk right back in. Seeing that he's indeed gone, I run over to my truck and pop the trunk. I quickly grab my luggage and bags and make my way back into the house. I lug everything down the stairs, to the basement door. I remove the key from my bra and place it in the lock; I'm so happy to hear the *click* when I turn the key! I push my way inside, turn on the light, and begin stuffing every bag I have to the brim with money.

Thirty minutes later, the bags are full and ready to be hauled outside. One by one, I struggle to carry them up the stairs and out the door. I'm out of breath and tired as hell by the time I secure the last one in my trunk. Who knew money weighs so damn much? My back and shoulders are hurting from the bag straps, and my legs are sore, but it's all worth it! Looking at the time, I see that I have at least forty-five minutes before he's due to return, so I run back downstairs. In the basement, I stack three pounds of kush on top of each other and place them inside my trunk as well. I don't smoke the shit myself, but being the businesswoman I am, I'll sure as hell find somebody who wants or needs it and is willing to pay for that shit. I'll sell it to them, and make an even bigger profit off of Angel's ass. I laugh at the thought as I walk out the door and head to my truck.

I slide my hands into black leather gloves and snap them at the wrist. I remove the small gas can from my truck and make my way back into the house. Starting from the basement, I pour a thin trail of gasoline leading up the stairs and into the kitchen. I don't use too much, because I ain't trying to burn the place to the ground; I only want to draw a little attention. I look around to make sure I haven't left anything important behind, and when I'm satisfied that I haven't, I continue the gas trail to the front door. Standing outside, I pull out a box of matches from my pocket, strike one, and toss it into the house. Instantly, the gasoline bursts into a line of flames.

I quickly make my way back to my truck, start it, and hurry out of the driveway. As I drive down the street, I can see the fire in my rearview mirror. Once I'm far enough down the street, I pull over on the side of the street and remove my gloves, which have my whole damn truck smelling like gasoline. I pick up my phone and make a call while I drive a bit farther, to a wooded area. I set the gloves and the gas can on fire there, as I don't want there to be any evidence to link me to theft and arson.

As I drive toward the freeway, a fire truck zooms by me, headed in the direction I just came from. *Damn, that was quick. I only called a few moments ago.*

With my truck full of money, I hop on the freeway and make my way home.

* * *

At my house, I place all the money bags in one of my spare rooms. I'm too tired to do anything else.

It's a little after 2:00 in the morning when I walk over to my iPad and pick it up, wanting to check out the 19 Action News app. I take a seat on my bed to look at it, and a smile spreads across my face when I read the headlines and know I got his ass: "Local Fire Brings Drug Bust." I play the video footage and hear an off-camera young Caucasian woman talking while

G Street Chronicles / 227

fire trucks, police cars, and people gather in front of what's left of Angel's house. I give the reporter my undivided attention when she begins to speak: "I'm Sandra Jiffy, and I'm standing on Old Pleasant Valley Road in Middleburg Heights, Ohio, where what started off as a house fire has ended in a local drug bust. Standing beside me is Chief Daniel Kozar. Chief, can you tell me what transpired here tonight?"

An older white man steps into the view of the camera and begins to talk. "We received a call that there was a fire going on. The Fire Department managed to get the blaze under control, but when they went inside to check the premises for survivors, they stumbled upon a basement full of marijuana and cash. As we were finishing up, a man walked up and told us this is his house, and he was immediately arrested and taking to the station for questioning. I'm not sure who set the house on fire, but it is clearly a case of arson, with gasoline as the cause. It's likely the arsonist was simply trying to make a statement or bring attention to the house, because effort was taken to make sure the entire place did not burn. Nevertheless, when we find the arsonist, he or she will be punished to the fullest extent of the law. Meanwhile, an investigation will be launched, and drug charges on the homeowner are likely."

"Thank you, Chief Kozar. As the chief said, the homeowner, a man by the name of Angel Rodriguez, was arrested tonight for the drugs and money confiscated from the house. If you have any tips that might help the police with the drug and/or arson investigation, please call Crime Stoppers. This is Sandra Jiffy, with 19 Action News. Back to you, Bob."

I damn near fall off the bed from laughing so hard, realizing my plan worked. When I pulled over to take off my gloves, I called 911 so they could make it to the house before it was too late. I knew the basement would be the last to burn, especially if they got there quick enough, so once they were inside the house, it was only a matter of time before they'd find all that contraband—enough to charge him several times over. Angel is a dumb ass for stopping though, because if it was me, ain't no way in the fuckin' world I'da walked up to the police and told them I lived there, knowing what I kept in the basement. I guess his brain's as tiny as his insignificant dick.

Climbing off the bed, I sit the iPad on the nightstand and walk into the bathroom. I turn on the shower and pin up my hair before placing my shower cap on top of my head. I remove my clothes, including my backward panties, and place them in a pile on the floor, then step into the shower. The water feels great against my skin as it washes the smell of gasoline off of my body. My back and shoulders are extremely sore from carrying all of those bags from the basement and up the stairs. Turning my back to the showerhead, I allow the massager to hit the most tender areas. I'm so sleepy that I don't know what to do with myself, so I decide to make this shower a quick one. I grab my loofah and lather it up with vanilla shower gel before rubbing it all over my body. Minutes later, I'm clean and stepping out of the shower, ready to make my way into my bedroom.

My body is still damp as I slide under the covers, but I don't even care. I rest my head on the pillow and close my eyes. A slight smile appears on my sleepy face. I'm rich, and I will be for the rest of my life! Happy thoughts take over my mind as I close my eyes and drift off to sleep.

CHAPTER 18

A loud noise wakes me out of my sleep, and I jump up before realizing it's a commercial on TV. I hate when that happens, and I wish I would have turned the damn thing off before I went to bed. I stretch and smile, still thinking about all the money I got from Angel's ass the night before last. I didn't wake up until late afternoon yesterday, so I got a later start. Once I finally did, I was up until 5 o'clock in the morning counting all of it; I'm still surprised at how much it was. Each plastic-wrapped package contained ten stacks of $1,000, all hundreds. I managed to walk away with twenty-eight of them, so I ended up with a whopping $280,000.

I know I can't take that shit to the bank, because they'll definitely lock my black ass up! I don't want that, so I stashed it all in the safe under the couch in my living room for safekeeping. I have plans to open a separate account and deposit little by little, until I have it all accounted for. I laugh to myself when I think about how Angel blew my phone up all that night and the entire day yesterday. I'm not sure how he did it from jail, but it was his ass, so of course I didn't answer. Still, that didn't stop him from leaving me all kinds of threatening messages, telling me what he's going to do to me when we cross paths. Half of them I couldn't understand because he was shooting that shit off in Spanish. I guess when he gets mad, that's all that comes out. Either way, I'm not the least bit worried, because he knows nothing about me. Even if he does, he has to get out of jail to do something, and as of today, his ass is still locked up.

Stretching, I glance over at the clock; it reads 11:30. I've got shit to do, so I climb out of bed. After doing my daily norm, I pick up my cell and dial McKenzie up.

"Hello?"

"Can I speak to McKenzie?"

"This is she."

"Oh, hey, girl! It's Brandy from the shop that day."

"My biggest customer!" She giggles. "What's up, girl?"

I hear a baby crying in the back ground as I ask, "Are you still going to the mall today?"

"Yeah. I'm about to get ready now. How about I call you when I'm about to leave?"

"That's cool. I'm about to get dressed also."

We disconnect the call, and I head into my closet.

Two hours later, I'm in the parking lot of Beachwood Mall, waiting for McKenzie. The plan is simple: We'll go inside, I'll show her everything I want, and she'll come back in and get it for me. At first she wanted to get the shit while I stood there, but after I told her ass I wasn't having that, we came up with this plan.

I hear a song I like on the mix CD that I bought the other day, and I turn the volume up: "My gun dirty, my brick clean. I'm riding dirty, my dick clean. She talk dirty, but her mouth clean. Bitch, I'm MC Hammer, I'm about cream." I sing along, bobbing my head to Rick Ross's song.

A tap on my window startles me, and I look over and see McKenzie smiling. "Damn, girl, you was jamming, wasn't you? I heard yo' shit bumping all the way in my car." She laughs after I roll my window down.

"Ricky is my baby with his fat ass! He could never get on top of me though, I would straight have to ride him. My life is too precious!"

"I know that's right."

We both laugh, and I roll up my window. I lock my truck up, and we head into the mall. I walk around and show McKenzie everything I want her to get, and she nods to let me know that she's got it. This silk St. John outfit catches my eye; it has me written all over it. It's a black one-piece short set that comes a little shorter than mid-thigh, with a scrunched waist. The deep, plunging neckline shows hella cleavage, but not so much that it looks trashy. It's sexy, yet elegant at the same time. The mannequin does it no justice, so I think it's only fair that I rock it the right way. I pick through the racks to make sure they have my size before I add it to my list. Grateful that they do, I summon McKenzie over toward me to show her. I simply must have this, and I want her to get it first so she doesn't forget. After I show her the outfit, she walks away, I'm assuming to pick up some merchandise for her other customers.

"Today must be my lucky day," I hear. The voice is so close that it feels like the person is standing directly behind me.

I turn around, startled, and damn near run into this tall, light-skinned chick's chest. I instantly get irritated, wondering why the fuck she's so close to me. Not wanting to ruin my shopping experience, I bite my tongue and step back in an attempt to move around her. She takes a step in the same direction as I do, blocking me. I step the other way, but she does the same thing again.

"Excuse me!" I say, my patience running thin.

"Naw, bitch" She laughs and takes a step closer to my face.

"What the fuck is your problem?" I ask, really confused as to why she's trying to get greasy in Saks.

Looking her over, I see that she looks familiar, but I can't pinpoint exactly where I know her from. She's dressed like a boy in those baggy Levi's denim shorts and a wife-beater. She's got French braids in her hair and tall as shit! She has to be about six-two, because I ain't short but with me being five-seven, with stiletto's on, we are standing eye to eye. Another girl is standing beside her, about my height, with blonde micro braids, dressed in a short skirt and stilettos. I quickly figure out that the light-skinned one is a dyke, and old girl in the skirt is probably her girlfriend.

"You don't remember me, do you?" she asks, so close I can smell the spearmint on her breath.

"Should I?"

"Naw, but you will after today."

I laugh to myself. *This ho is some kind of character.* "Yeah, I hear ya. Girl, bye. I got shit to do." I attempt to push past her, but she puts her arm out, blocking my path. I release air out of my nose in frustration, realizing that this situation is quickly about to turn psychical.

"Where the hell are you going?"

I take a step back and glare at her, my way of letting her know she has one more muthafucking time to put her hands on me before it's on!

"Why you play my cousin like that?"

"Who is yo' cousin?" I ask, still having no clue who she is or what the hell she's talking about.

"What, you don't remember babysitting Sade's kids? If I remember correctly, that was the day you fucked up her life. I'm her cousin, Meka."

I laugh loudly in her face. I remember the boy-looking bitch now, and it's all starting to make sense. "You're coming at me all crazy over that bum?" I crack up. "I ain't fuck up nobody's life. Her life was in shambles when I met her broke ass, so why don't you get the fuck outta here with that dumb shit? I ain't thinking about you or that ho."

"You got one more time to say some slick shit about my blood before I put you on yo' ass!" she snarls.

Her girlfriend—or whoever the fuck the micro braid chick is—moves from beside me and stands behind me.

These hoes must think I'm a sucka or something, coming at me the way they are. I don't know if it's my gear or what that makes them think I'm a pushover or something. Don't these bitches know I can still throw these things, even in six-inch stilettos. If they don't, they will very soon. I laugh again. This shit is hilarious! Micro Braids thinks she's slick, but I'm far from a dummy. She may not know it, but she's still in my vision. As soon as she makes a move, I'm dropping her ass!

"What's funny?" Meka asks, mean-mugging me.

I smirk, not giving her a reply before I blast her right in the face with all my might. She staggers back a few steps but gains control pretty quick and starts coming toward me. I post up, backing myself against the closest wall, preparing for whatever. If these bitches think jumping me gon' be easy, they got another thing coming. Micro Braids runs up and throws two weak-ass jabs. I block them both and return a shot right to her eye, hard enough to make the ho see stars.

Meka runs back up with her guards up, and we square off.

She throws a punch, and I feel my lip split and start to bleed. Pissed, I throw a few and connect. Once again, she staggers back, and I go in for the kill, swinging with everything in me. I hit her with solid jabs from left to right, trying my best to knock the big bitch out. She grabs hold of my hair, and we lock up. Using all my weight, I push her up against the wall. When she's stuck, with nowhere else to go, I begin raining punches down, all over the top of her head. My head jerks back, and it hurts like hell, but I don't allow it to stop me from putting the hurt on Meka's big ass.

"Bitch, get the fuck off her!" I hear McKenzie scream, and I instantly feel relief.

Using Meka's braids as leverage, I push her head down and deliver uppercuts with my right hand while keeping her steady with my left. She swings wildly, hitting me in the face a few times, but she doesn't do any real damage, because I'm bobbing and ducking most of them. Between every swing, I draw my fist back and come up full force, tagging her all in her shit. Planting the bottoms of my stilettos to the floor firmly, I put both my hands in her hair and swing her left and right, throwing her ass right into a clothing rack. It makes a loud crashing sound as it falls to the floor, causing a domino effect on a few of the others. She lies there without moving, and I take this time to run over to where McKenzie is kicking ol' girl's ass. There are micro braids all over the floor, and even though McKenzie is already winning, I step in and throw a few punches just for some get-back.

"Break it up! Break it up!" a baritone voice yells.

It takes six security guards to break up both fights, because no one wants to stop. They drag us all into this small office, daring any of us to move. After looking at a videotape of the assault, the police are called, and they escort Meka and her girlfriend, Tessa, out of the building first, telling McKenzie and me to wait. They warn us that the next time something like this happens, we'll be banned from the mall and arrested. I am so fucking embarrassed. Who in the hell has an all-out brawl in Saks? I'm praying that nobody finds out about this shit, because I wouldn't even know how to explain it.

Back outside, on the way to my truck, I stop at McKenzie's car. "Thanks, girl. I really appreciate it," I tell her truthfully.

"You're welcome. I can't stand when bitches try to jump somebody. If you're too scared to fight one on one, what the hell are you fighting for?" She laughs. She has a small scratch on her forehead, and her hair is not in a ponytail anymore, but that's about it.

"Right. I hate an ol' scary ho!" I chime in.

"What were y'all fighting for anyway?" she asks as she unlocks her door, preparing to get in.

"If I give you a reason, I'll be lying. All she said to me was that I played her cousin. Other than that, I got no clue."

"Damn. Well, she got her ass whooped for her cousin then!" We both burst out laughing.

"I'll be back before the week is out to get your stuff. I'll call you when you when I have everything."

"That sounds good to me. Thank you again," I say as I walk away, headed for my truck.

Climbing into the driver seat, I shake my head, amazed by what just happened. I can't believe I actually had a fucking fistfight in the damn mall, like some common 'hood rat. I'm pissed at that ho for coming at me the way she did, but I'm even more pissed that I let her get me out my hook-up in the first place. Securing my seatbelt, I stick my key in the ignition and start my truck.

Tired of thinking about the dumb-ass fight, I turn the radio back up and pull out of the parking space. As I continue down Cedar, my cell phone rings from a private number. I stare down at it but refuse to answer, knowing it could be any of a number of haters. I've had enough drama for one day, and I'm not gonna let anyone fuck up the rest of it.

When I make a left onto Euclid, I look in my rearview mirror and notice a Cadillac Seville doing the same. Usually, that wouldn't stand out, but that car's been following me since I left the mall. It's a dark metallic blue—so dark that it's almost black. The windows are tinted, making it impossible to see inside. From what I can see through the windshield, there are two, maybe three people inside.

A short time later, I make a right and begin to drive down Shaw, and I see the car do the same. I begin to slow down, in hopes that the driver will go around, but it continues the same speed as me; something's gotta give.

Creeped the fuck out, I put my hazard lights on and pull to a complete stop. Before I get a chance to shift into park, I'm rammed from the back by the Seville. My head jerks forward, and my horn beeps from the impact. I instantly hit the gas and speed off, heading down the street. The Seville gives chase, ramming my truck a few more times. Racing down Shaw, I hit speeds of seventy miles and hour as I maneuver my truck past the cars around me. Some of them beep their horns out of frustration, but I don't give a shit; somebody is trying to kill me! Checking the rearview mirror, I see the Seville picking up speed, ready to hit me once again, so I make a hard right and head up St. Clair.

"Nooo!" I scream when the Seville does the same and

pulls up beside me.

Fear grips my body as I witness a person in the back seat rolling down the window and pointing a huge gun at me. I can't see the person, but multiple shots ring out as I try to get away. I duck and dodge the bullets the best I can, but it's hard to do that and drive at the same time. In a panic, I jerk my wheel to the right and succeed in hitting the front of the Seville, causing them to swerve and almost hit a telephone pole. In no time, the driver takes control of the wheel, and they begin to follow me again. Bullets whiz by as I drive from lane to lane, praying to God that none of them hit me. My back window shatters, and I wonder how much ammo they've got. While trying to look back, my truck clips the back of a Mustang, causing it to spin out of control and hit the fire hydrant.

Tears are streaming down my face because I'm not ready to die. More shots ring out as I hit a left, heading up 152nd Street. My truck is beginning to resemble Swiss cheese from all the bullet holes. A bullet whizzes by my head and hits the rearview mirror, causing it to explode. Small pieces of glass and plastic fly everywhere, some hitting me in the face. I scream out in pain when I feel a piece cut into my cheek. As I speed up the street, cars attempt to get out of my way, and people on the street try to take cover. I'm trying to drive as best I can, ducking my head down. Where the fuck are the police when you need them?

Yanking my wheel, I put my truck up on two wheels and make a sharp left onto Lakeshore. As I continue to drive down the street, I realize I don't hear any more gunshots. Lifting my head a bit and using the side mirrors, I see that the Seville is no longer behind me. I take my foot off the gas and slow down a bit to check out my surroundings. Frantically, I look around, looking for the car or any sign of danger. I don't see anything out of the ordinary, and I'm starting to wonder what the hell happened to the Seville. When I'm satisfied that I'm no longer being followed, I'm finally able to breathe.

As I continue to drive, I continue to look around for the Seville. It seems odd that it just stopped chasing me. Again, I don't see any sign of it, and I'm grateful. I'm forced to stop at a light, and drop my head into my chest and close my eyes, thanking God. A horn behind me blares, and I hit the gas. No sooner than I do this, I start to feel a burning sensation in my back and chest. Trying to pay attention to the road, I glance down and see that the front of my black tank top is wet. I touch it with my hand and pull it back, only to find it covered with blood. The burning continues. Panic takes over my body, and my breathing becomes shallow. Every minute, it's getting harder and harder to breathe.

"I've been shot! That muthafucka shot me!" I scream as best I can, but it's hard.

My vision blurs, and it's hard for me to see. I hear horns beeping and honking around me, but I don't know why. The wind is knocked out of me as my truck jerks forward, causing the air bags to deploy. It sounds as if metal is crushing. Someone walks over to my truck window and asks me if I'm all right, but I don't reply because I can't. I begin to see shades of red, blue, and yellow as I fade in and out of consciences. So many thoughts run through my mind as I try to figure out who did this to me. I've fucked so many people over in such a short amount of time, so I have no clue. The burning in my chest and back is replaced with a feeling of numbness.

Visions of my life flash before my eyes. I remember my mother calling me ugly and slapping me in the face for no reason at all. I recall the men from my neighborhood, humping me on our old, ratty couch. I even remember that horrible fight with my mother before I took her life and Pitch telling me he was going to treat me like a princess. I also remember his ass putting me out on the ho stroll, making me—his own daughter—sell my body. Trixie's beautiful face comes to mind, and she looks the way she used to at first, but then her face is all cut up and disfigured, just like it was after Pitch finished with her. Tears roll down my face when I recall the night Xavier cooked dinner for me, the night before he walked out of my life. Suddenly, a series of familiar faces flashes by one by one, faster and faster: Osha, Taz, Sade, Meka, Angel, and Roger. Then they all disappear, and I know that I just saw a lineup: Any of them could have done this.

Through my blurry eyes, I see someone struggling to open my door. People are talking to me, but I can't hear a word they're saying. Everything moves in slow motion as my eyes roll back in my head. I say a silent prayer to God, asking that He'll allow me into the pearly gates. I've lived in hell my entire life, so it would be nice if I could get a taste of heaven for once. My body begins to shake, and there's nothing I can do to stop it. The violent shivering lasts for only a few moments, then ends as quickly as it started. Suddenly, everything is calm. I no longer feel pain. I only feel free, and then…everything goes black…

To Be Continued…
Heartless 2: Still Grimy
Coming Soon

We'd like to thank you for supporting G Street Chronicles and invite you to join our social networks. Please be sure to post a review when you're finished reading.

Facebook
G Street Chronicles Fan Page
G Street Chronicles CEO Exclusive Readers Group

Twitter
@GStreetChronicl

Email us and we'll add you to our mailing list
fans@gstreetchronicles.com

George Sherman Hudson, CEO
Shawna A., COO